E 90346

This book is to be returned to the issuing library not later than the last date shown. Fines will be levied if a book is overdue. Senior citizens and the disabled are exempt from paying fines.

16 AUG 1991	16 OCT 1993	22 MAR 1997
-6 SEP 1991	18 DEC 1993	20 OCT 1997
15 NOV 1991	-9 FEB 1994	-1 DEC 1997
-6 FEB 1992	-2 DEC 1994	24 DEC 1997
-2 APR 1992	31 MAY 1995	
27 APR 1992	10 JUL 1995	
20 JUL 1992	28 AUG 1995	
12 AUG 1992	27 NOV 1995	
24 AUG 1992	-4 MAY 1996	
-5 SEP 1992	-6 AUG 1996	
7 DEC 1992	-7 NOV 1996	
	23 NOV 1996	
1- JUL 1993		
11 OCT 1993	22 FEB 1997	

KILMARNOCK & LOUDOUN DISTRICT LIBRARIES

Flying High

Hang-gliding is a dangerous sport. When Ben Turpin, Glasgow art dealer and former colleague of Jarvis, dies in a publicity stunt on Ben Lomond, Jarvis, who is employed on unspecified government service, is asked by his employer to liaise with the police investigation because he had recently re-established contact with Turpin.

Inspector Cohen of the Glasgow Police and Jarvis find that the widow, the ex-wife (a former friend of Jarvis's) and a French art dealer all have more than a normal interest in the death, and Turpin himself may have been involved in the recent deaths of some of those close to him.

With the help of a Parisian salon assistant, an explanation is found, but things are more complicated than they seem. One thing is clear: those who would fly high should take care not to fall.

by the same author

THE CROAKING OF THE RAVEN
DEATH AND THE REMEMBRANCER
A DEATH IN TIME

FRANCIS LYALL

Flying High

THE CRIME CLUB
An Imprint of HarperCollins *Publishers*

First published in Great Britain in 1991
by The Crime Club, an imprint of
HarperCollins Publishers, 77–85 Fulham Palace Road,
Hammersmith, London W6 8JB

Francis Lyall asserts the moral right to be identified
as the author of this work.

© Francis Lyall 1991

British Library Cataloguing in Publication Data

Lyall, Francis
 Flying high.—(Crime Club)
 I. Title
 823.914

ISBN 0 00 232341 9

Photoset in Linotron Baskerville by
Rowland Phototypesetting Ltd
Bury St Edmunds, Suffolk
Printed and bound in Great Britain by
HarperCollins Book Manufacturing, Glasgow

For my Mother,
with love
and thanks

CHAPTER 1

September

'I don't like that one,' Jarvis said decisively, gesturing with his free hand to the picture hanging beside the woman. It was a large oil painting, about six feet by four, and they were so close to it that its gouts of paint stood out in relief.

'Do you know much about painting?' she asked coolly. 'Or are you one of those "I know what I like/like what I know" people?'

Jarvis shrugged. 'I've been through a lot of galleries in my time,' he said noncommittally.

'You sound like a much travelled exhibition.' Her tone was arch.

The surrounding group laughed politely.

'Come now, Imogen,' said a lanky individual, 'you and Ben wouldn't make a living, let alone finance your lifestyle, if there weren't a lot of us about who know what we like and are willing to pay for it.'

She laughed prettily. 'I suppose that's true, Jeremy. But it's no reason not to encourage a knowledge of art as well as a simple liking for some painters. If one really *knows* art, the pleasure one gets from excellence is immeasurably increased.' She gazed intently at Jeremy, eyes flashing. Under her gaze the young man seemed to bloom.

Jarvis bit his lip. Imogen! He had been getting close to quarrelling with his host's wife: or at least that was how it seemed. It was unlikely there was more than one Imogen at the reception. 'Imogen's somewhere about. I'll introduce you later,' Ben Turpin had said.

Jarvis stood, silenced. In ordinary circumstances he might well have waded in with the suggestion that people who prattled about 'knowing art' seemed usually to have the oddest standards of 'excellence'. To him such were self-congratulatory gnostics, an 'in-group' bound only by their shared pretensions to knowledge. But now! He could hardly argue with Imogen Turpin. After all, he was merely a guest at the gala opening of the new Turpin Gallery.

He looked about. Might there be some way to escape? He was starting to feel trapped. She was well-built, with long flowing silver-blonde dyed hair—statuesque was the adjective the tabloids would use—and opinionated. The curse of it was that she was pleasant with it as well. He reckoned she must be a good saleswoman.

The Gallery was well-appointed, he considered. It was oddly shaped in that it had two waists, one immediately behind the window area where it was made by a counter. The other was farther back, designed to set apart the area where the real business was done, the place where the owner entertained those who had the cash to buy. The Gallery walls were different colours, a muddy deep red forming the backcloth for nineteenth-century work, while pastel grey and a faint aquamarine were used for the moderns. There was nothing very early on show.

He fidgeted. Imogen Turpin had now placed herself just too far forward for him to adjourn from the group gracefully. He was about to be ungraceful when Ben came to the rescue, beaming his way into the group, his glasses twinkling in the lights. He was a large man, and Jarvis immediately remembered one of his nicknames: Big Ben.

'I didn't really expect you to come,' Turpin said to Jarvis. 'I'm glad you and Imogen are getting on together.' He slipped his arm round his wife and gave her a squeeze. Expertly, she freed herself.

'He doesn't like your prize picture,' she said, turning to look at it.

'Rubbish,' stated Turpin. 'It's a masterpiece. Wouldn't part with it for anything under a fiver.' He grinned broadly.

Jarvis looked again at the picture.

It was of Icarus—Icarus falling. It was executed in blocks—almost slabs—of paint, with a bold use of black to delineate the patches of colour. Behind and above the melting wings and the figure of the boy the sun-god drove his chariot across the heavens. Low to the right, the shocked figure of Daedalus winged his way to safety. Low to the left, the waves awaited the falling, foolish boy. There was a rocky shore to the right, and in the distance a boat bobbed on the restless sea. The picture was crude, yet there was something about it. He didn't like it, but the recesses of Jarvis's mind threw up a label.

'The New Glasgow School?' he asked.

'Good. Good. That's very good,' said Turpin heartily, clapping Jarvis on the back. 'He knows more than he lets on,' he added to the general group. 'He was always like that,' he added to his wife.

She sipped her drink, eyeing Jarvis over its rim. He had the impression that she was reassessing him.

'Come on now,' said Turpin to Jarvis. 'How's your glass?' He seized it and bore it briefly off. The group, sensing that two old acquaintances had just met, melted away. Other people's reminiscences are not always interesting.

'I'm glad you could come,' Turpin said as he brought back the glass recharged. 'I only sent the invitation on the off-chance. A mutual friend gave me your address, and, well—hell, we were good friends.' He looked Jarvis in the face.

Jarvis responded with a smile. It was true. They had been good friends. But then there had been the matter of Lynn, and soon after Ben had been posted elsewhere with his new wife and they had drifted out of touch. Ben had left the Foreign Service, and after that Jarvis had heard little of him. The marriage had failed. Jarvis himself had 'gone civilian', and then a few weeks ago, out of the blue had come the invitation to the 'Grand Opening of the Turpin Gallery' with 'Do Come' written in Turpin's unmistakable hand across its front.

'Just like you,' went on Turpin. 'Casting asparagus at a prized possession. He's got a wicked sense of humour,' he added to his wife. 'Do you know,' he went on, 'this fellow's a great practical joker? I remember one flight from Geneva with him. You know how the pilots sometimes send round a note of where we're going, what height and speed and so on?'

She nodded.

'Well, he put it in his pocket, took another one from a different flight out and sent it round. I forget what it was. We were going to London, and I think the one you produced—' he turned back to Jarvis—'was for a flight to Rome?'

Jarvis shrugged.

'It caused an awful stink,' continued Turpin. 'One bloke thought he was on the wrong flight! Got hold of the stewardess and complained.' He began to laugh loudly.

Jarvis glanced about, embarrassed, but no one seemed to pay any attention.

'I remember something else you used to do.' Turpin recovered himself. 'You used to buy flight insurance at the airport and make it payable to the oddest persons. You once made it payable to the Chancellor of the Exchequer!' He guffawed.

Jarvis smiled. He still did that sort of thing. It gave him a curious feeling on take-off to know that if there were a disaster, someone, often a charity, would gain an unexpected benefit.

'You'll need to excuse me,' said Imogen Turpin suddenly. 'There's Tessa.' She moved away.

'How's Ben?' Jarvis asked Turpin once she was out of earshot.

Turpin's face changed. The grin vanished and he frowned slightly. 'He's OK. So far as I can see, but that's not much.'

'Difficult, is it?'

'I see him once a month, for an afternoon. Oh, I've got the right to take him for a fortnight every summer, but . . .' He sighed. 'I've lost touch with him, I suppose. Besides, I'm not sure Imogen likes seeing him around. Reminds her she's not the first Mrs Turpin, I suppose.'

'And Lynn?'

'Don't know.'

'I'm intrigued that you've moved into the art business,'

said Jarvis, waving generally at the Gallery and the surrounding groups. 'It must take a lot of capital.'

The words were statement, but Turpin correctly saw the question behind them. 'Diplomatic as ever,' he said, grinning. 'What you mean is: how does a consistent near-bankrupt like me get the money to get into the business? The answer is,' he went on, giving Jarvis no chance to demur, 'that we've come into a little money, me and the wife.'

'Good for you. I hope it works.' Jarvis sipped his drink. 'And how's life otherwise?'

Turpin suddenly gave a wolfish grin. Jarvis recognized it. If the grin was anything to go by, Turpin was still at his old tricks. Jarvis himself had suffered from Turpin's dedicated womanizing, so he did not want to know now. He swiftly changed the subject.

'I like some of what's here, but not all of it. This, for example,' he said, turning back to the picture. He stepped back a pace or two, head on one side.

'Come on,' Turpin encouraged. 'There must be something good about it. Others have praised it.'

'I suppose the cloud's OK.' Jarvis was hesitant. 'But I'd not like to swim in that.' He pointed a finger at the wind-swept sea.

'D'you still swim?'

'No. Not really. You?'

'A bit, since we came north. You know, I still remember those lifesaving classes we went to. And old Wally—Wally the Walrus. He trained us pretty good, didn't he?'

'Mm.' Jarvis was noncommittal. He was always cautious when people started reminiscing, for he had found that his recollection and theirs did not always coincide. 'I do like the framing,' he remarked, to change the subject back to the picture. 'So many pictures are ruined by their frames.'

'That's true,' said Turpin. 'We're careful about our frames.'

'Do you do your own?'

'Imogen does it. She's good with her hands. Me? I'm a bit handless.'

11

'Yes. I remember that,' said Jarvis, nodding wryly.

'But Imogen does a good job. And our pictures are worth every penny. Come. See.' Turpin ushered him across to another wall full of pictures. 'Look.' He pointed at one, and putting a hand into his pocket took out another pair of glasses, which he swapped with the ones on his nose. '*Winter Scene*,' he said, reading the card.

Then he saw Jarvis's look, and flourished the glasses in his hand. 'Yes. I'm afraid I need two pairs now. One to read and for close work. The others for ordinary seeing.'

'Why don't you try bifocals?'

'I did. I did. But it wouldn't work. I couldn't get adjusted—fell downstairs and suchlike. Besides, one needs to see a picture through the whole lens, not a strip at the foot.'

Jarvis inspected the picture. It was unremarkable.

Just then an elderly woman—an Elderly Personage—approached.

'Mr Turpin,' she shrilled while still some distance away. 'I am *so* delighted with your new Gallery . . .'

'I'll go see the rest of the exhibition,' Jarvis said hurriedly. 'May see you later, but if not, thanks for the invitation.'

'OK,' said Turpin. 'Hope to see you later on, but if not, do remember where we are. Come and spend some money. Contribute to my old age pension.' He turned to the old woman. 'Mrs Gray, I'm so pleased you were able to come. I understood from Molly that you'd not been too well recently.'

To escape the ensuing protestations of health, Jarvis gave his attention once more to the picture. He still didn't like it.

He turned to the other pictures. Towards the door he saw Imogen Turpin speaking to an attractive golden-blonde woman dressed in black, presumably Tessa. The woman turned and Jarvis saw the two were unmistakably sisters. They had the same forehead, eyes, nose, jaw and cheek structure. Clinically he checked off the correspondences.

'It's rude to stare,' said a voice in his ear.

'Am I?' asked Jarvis, turning to meet a slight smile on the face of a stranger.

that you should be told that he painted the picture himself, and that he hoped you would prize it accordingly.'

'He painted it?' Jarvis began to laugh.

'I believe so.' The lawyer, offended by Jarvis's reaction, clearly expected some explanation or apology but Jarvis did not gratify him.

Jarvis got to his feet. 'Well, thanks for your help,' he said. 'I take it that I can write to you shortly about the picture?'

'I believe that the widow would like to move it out soon, but I dare say she could hang on to it for a few days till you get things sorted out at home. It is quite big.'

'It's all of that,' said Jarvis abstractedly.

'I can't say I liked it when I saw it myself,' observed the lawyer.

Jarvis held out his hand. 'I might agree.' He smiled.

The lawyer suddenly smiled in return as he shook Jarvis's hand, a smile that had a lurking warmth in it, Jarvis felt. Perhaps he had made some progress after all.

'I'll get back to you about it,' Jarvis promised.

The lawyer showed them out, omitting to shake Cohen's hand.

'Odd bloke,' said Jarvis as they went down the stairs.

Cohen nodded. 'There's reasons.'

They went out on to the street. Cohen continued. 'He's not a police fan—not in the least.'

'Why?'

'It's a long time ago. Before I was on the Force. Apparently he had a daughter. She was lifted by a car on her way home from school.'

Jarvis felt a cold chill run down his spine.

'She was found two days later. Dead. They got a man after that, but because of some police error the trial was abandoned. He's been bitter about police ever since.'

'Poor man. I can see his point. But wouldn't that lead him to help rather than hinder?'

'Could have gone both ways, I suppose. But rumour has it that the man in charge of the case was off-hand with him when they met after the trial broke up. He should have apologized, but . . .' Cohen shrugged. 'Had something else on his mind, I suppose. Whatever—he greatly offended.'

CHAPTER 5

Thursday

Some minutes after eleven the next morning Jarvis drew his car into the driveway of Ben Turpin's home, Buena Vista. It was a modern detached house, of the style where an angled roof projects over both ends and the pitch of the roof runs from front to back. It was discreet: not too large, but giving just a suggestion of 'money'.

The tarmac to the right of the house led to a parking area in front of a large single-doored double garage at the back of the garden. A wire fence divided the parking place from its mirror image belonging to the house next door. Jarvis parked, blew out his cheeks a couple of times and got out of the car. He wasn't sure that he was looking forward to this interview, and was annoyed with himself for being late. He always felt at a disadvantage if he was not punctual for an appointment.

On the other side of the fence a woman was bending over plants. She straightened, moving her head to allow the breeze to blow her hair out of her eyes. High cheekbones and dark hair made her an attractive picture.

'Hi,' she said.

''Morning,' Jarvis replied.

As he came round the corner to the front door he saw the view. The house deserved its name. The centre of five architect-designed houses set on a hillside north-west of Bearsden over towards Drymen. The house itself faced south. Beyond the far end of the house he could see the rising hills, and, he thought, the half-hidden cone of Ben Lomond peering over the shoulders of its courtiers.

Imogen Turpin opened the door as he approached.

'I heard the car,' she said. 'Mr Jarvis, isn't it?'

'I'm sorry I'm late,' he replied. 'I got lost.' This was not entirely accurate. He had deliberately left Glasgow early intending to see what it was like where Ben Turpin had finally settled. However, he had got on to a narrow road which had taken him over the hill on which Turpin's house was situated before he was able to find a place to turn.

'It's easy to get lost round here,' she said, holding out her hand. 'These small roads. Come in.'

Her grip was strong, and the handshake expert, drawing him past her and into the house. Although Jarvis himself was not small, as he remembered she was taller, but her silver-blonde hair was now gold. He was unprepared for her to be wearing a white dress with a large flower pattern. It did not seem right for a recent widow. Other than that, she was the person he remembered.

'That way.' She gestured to an open door at the left which led into a lounge with wide picture windows. The single one in the west wall had a curtain drawn over it.

She saw him notice that. 'It is the best view,' she said as she sat in an armchair beside the fireplace, 'but I can't face it yet.'

'I understand,' he said, sitting at the far end of the leather sofa.

He glanced around. The carpet was Persian, the chairs and sofa cocoa-brown leather. The walls were the same red as the Turpin Gallery, and on them hung several pictures. Occasional tables held expensive porcelain. More curios were in a display cabinet in an alcove to the side of a wide fireplace on the short wall. In the alcove at the other side stood a rolltop desk. It was closed, but an overstuffed Filofax stood on top of it between two pieces of porcelain.

'We occasionally bring—brought—particular clients out to see pictures in a domestic setting,' she said quietly.

'I'm sorry I wasn't able to write before the funeral,' he began awkwardly. 'And that wasn't the best time to introduce myself. But, as I said on the phone, we did meet once before. At the opening of the Gallery last year.'

She shrugged. 'There were so many notes and cards. I didn't take in who wrote and who didn't. Some I'd heard of or knew. Others . . .' She opened her hands, then looked narrowly at him. 'Yes. I do recall. You're the one that didn't like Ben's picture. And, if I'm not mistaken, Ben has left the damned thing to you.'

'So I understand,' replied Jarvis, wondering whether he ought to test whether she would prefer to keep Ben's picture herself. He decided to leave that question for the present. 'I don't know why he'd do such a thing. Unless it's his sense of humour. I knew your husband from years back. We were students together at Greyhavens,' he continued. 'But he maybe filled you in about that.'

'Yes.' Her tone was low.

'Ben and I were good friends once, but latterly we had lost track. My fault, I suppose. I was never good at writing—or phoning.' He looked out of the window. 'Did he ever say anything about before he went into the art business?'

'Not really.' She shifted in her seat.

'Pity. We had great times together.'

'He never said much about the time before we met.'

'Where did you meet, may I ask?'

'London.' She shifted in her seat and picked a cigarette from an onyx box and, when Jarvis made no move, lit it from an onyx and gilt table lighter.

'You met professionally?'

'Yes. Ben was starting in business for himself, and we met at an auction. I'd seen him before that, but . . .' She shrugged, letting the initial smoke drift from her mouth.

'If London, why did you come up here?'

She smiled. 'His first idea was to have two galleries, one here and one in London, but I persuaded him that was crazy. Besides, we'd have had to live apart, and I wasn't for that.' She blew an expressive puff of smoke into the air.

'But why Glasgow?'

'You don't know much about art,' she observed shrewdly.

Jarvis shrugged, affecting ignorance.

She tapped her cigarette into an ashtray. 'Glasgow's been really undersold. The boorish drunks. The "ba'heids", they call them. Those awful images of the Gorbals, the Depression and so on. They've taken years to dissipate.'

Jarvis nodded. 'I suppose that's true. "Glaswegian" doesn't drag up a pleasant picture, even with that "Glasgow's Miles Better" slogan.'

'Quite. And say "Glasgow" and you certainly wouldn't think of something artistic. But go back to Charles Rennie Mackintosh. And before that there's Glasgow the Second City of the Empire, the manufacturing barons, the railways and heavy industry, shipping and such-like. They made money. You can see it still in the Victorian buildings. And some of it went into art. Some of it's in the collections. Some's still in the families.'

'I see what you mean,' said Jarvis slowly. 'I've been to the Burrell. But even given all that, Glasgow wouldn't seem to me to be a likely place to set up a gallery in the . . . was it the nineteen-seventies?'

'Early 'eighty-two. August Nineteen Eighty-two. The Turpin Gallery.' She rose to her feet grandly as she spoke, then relaxed. 'Would you like a drink?'

He nodded.

'Whisky? Gin? Sherry? . . .'

'I'm driving. It'd better be something like a dry ginger ale.'

'You're not serious!'

'I am.'

She flashed a glance at him, and recognized something in his eyes.

When she came back she carried on as if there had been no interruption.

'It went well. So well we were able to open the new place last year.'

'Were you surprised?'

She ignored the question. 'All that Victorian money and interest in art produced some excellent collections round here, you know. There's the Whistlers in the University . . . though the godawful philistines up there threatened to sell them some years back to get themselves out of a hole.' She took a pull at her large gin and tonic.

'While you were out my memory went to work. Am I

right that there's been some sort of a "Glasgow School" of young artists developed these last few years?' Jarvis asked.

'Yes. Exactly. There was all that talent lying about undeveloped and unexploited—at least, it was when we were setting up.'

'And that's why you picked Glasgow.'

'The alternative was Edinburgh.' She shrugged eloquently.

'But you foresaw what was going to happen.'

'No. I wouldn't pretend we saw it coming that clearly, but it seemed like a good bet, and, bluntly, I have an older sister here who was aware of what was going on artistically. That reduced the odds somewhat.'

'So you persuaded Ben.' He sipped his ginger ale.

'He didn't need much persuading. He never liked the London crowd. Neither did I.'

'I know what you mean. But that could be more cultural than substance. Maybe they're naturally shallow down there?' He smiled.

She laughed, and tapped more ash off her cigarette. Then she looked up, quite expressionless. 'But you've not come here for a seminar in how to start in on the art racket.'

'It is a racket, is it?'

She nodded, and waited for him to respond to her own implied question.

'I'm here in part because there is some concern about Ben's death.'

She looked at the end of her cigarette. The smoke curled upward.

'Concern?'

'Concern.'

There was another brief silence before Jarvis resumed. 'At one time in his career Ben was involved with matters of some delicacy. Sudden deaths are always a matter of concern when that's the case.'

'The police have been here.'

'I know.'

'You're not with the police.' The tone made it more of a statement than a question.

'Not in the usual sense of "with".'

'I see.' She ground out her cigarette, got up and crossed to the window. The brightness outside made a halo of her hair.

'You don't seem surprised,' he offered.

'Somehow I'm not,' she replied, turning back to face him. Then she went back to her seat and lit another cigarette. 'You asked whether Ben ever spoke about your times together. Has this something to do with his time before . . . before Ben and I met?' she finished with a rush.

'That would be the basis of the concern that led to my being asked to come and talk to you. At least, that sounds very formal. I was to be in the area in any case.' Jarvis found himself prevaricating. He wondered why.

'I see. Or rather, I don't. What am I supposed to do now? Do I ask you for identification? Or is that only when you've got someone at the door? You're in already. Or do you carry any identification?'

'You could phone Inspector Cohen if you like and check I'm genuine.'

She cracked a brief laugh. 'Cohen!' She stubbed out her cigarette and lit another. 'What d'you need to know? I've nothing to hide, though you're beginning to make me think Ben had.'

Jarvis spread his hands and shrugged. 'It'll be enough if I just ask some questions. I dare say the police have already covered the ground, but I need to ask these matters independently.'

'They were horrible.'

'How so?'

'They didn't say anything direct. Not at first. They asked about how Ben went about preparing for his damned hang-gliding—as if I knew! He used to do all that with his friends in the garage out there.' She waved a hand towards the other end of the house. 'Then at the end of the evening they'd come back in here and get drunk.' She took another pull at her drink.

'And then? The police, I mean.'

'They said something had gone wrong with the glider—

as though that was mysterious. Any fool could see that from the evening news pictures.' She shook her head, her hair cascading over her face, then she swept it back and stared at him. 'It was always a risk . . . trusting yourself to something like that bundle of wire and nylon.' She stubbed out her part-smoked cigarette. 'But one of them began to ask things about how the business was going. And how we were getting on together. You know . . . sex, that sort of thing.' Her hands were in her lap, the knuckles whitening. Then she covered her face. Jarvis went over to her, and she sobbed against his side.

At length she quietened.

'Shall I go?' he asked.

'No.' She fumbled another cigarette from the pack and lit it. 'I'm all right now. Let's get it over with.'

He looked carefully at her. Her gaze was steady. So were her hands as she inhaled smoke and let it trickle from her nose.

'OK. But I'll probably have to repeat things you've already told the police.'

She shrugged.

'The traditional question would be, "Had Ben any enemies?"' He spoke lightly, running a finger down the condensation on his glass.

'No more than most, so far as I know.'

'What sort of enemies did he have?'

'The usual. Anyone in the art world has a few folk they can't stand. Sometimes it's because they managed to put one over on you. Sometimes it's . . .' She hesitated, looking for words. 'Stealing clients. I suppose that's the worst.'

'You mean that Ben was good at putting one over on his competitors? And at stealing clients?' Jarvis confidently expected the answer to both elements—that was the Ben he had known.

She nodded.

'But that's not enough to explain someone killing him, if that's what happened.'

'Why not?' She looked across at the window.

'Do feelings run that deep? Are art folk capable of that

kind of planning? It's one thing to run someone down with a car, say, given the chance. It's quite another to sabotage a hang-glider. That's too deliberate.' He picked up his glass.

She sat silent, watching the smoke rise from the cigarette. 'I hadn't thought of that,' she replied at last. Then she pulled herself together, stubbed out the cigarette and sat erect, looking confidently at Jarvis.

She took up her glass and finished her gin and tonic. 'Of course, there's no reason to think someone killed him. He'd done a repair on the damned glider and got it wrong. When could someone have got at the thing? How come Ben didn't notice if someone had interfered with it?'

Jarvis sat a moment in thought. 'Well, you've already said the glider was out in the garage. Someone could've got in at night, say. Or was the garage locked?'

'That's true,' she said slowly. 'In fact, we never shut the garage during the day, normally. The first one out opened the door and the last one in shut it.' She went to the window once more, and stood looking out. 'There was no need. There was nothing in the garage, and you can't see it from the road.'

'There was the glider.'

'Flat against the wall—out of the way of the cars.'

'From what you say, the door was shut at night.'

She nodded.

'And locked?'

'Of course—at least usually.'

'And was it open in the days immediately before the . . . the . . .'

She swung round. 'The accident which you're thinking may be murder?'

'I'm not saying it was murder. I'm just tossing theories around.'

'Like hell you are. You said just now jealousy in the art world didn't seem enough to explain someone killing him. You're meaning the glider was tampered with, aren't you?' Her voice rose.

'That isn't clear. It may be that there was some latent weakness. Or it might be Ben made a mistake and used a wire with too low a breaking strain when making modifications or repairs. You say he had done repairs to the thing?'

'Yes. At least twice.' She came and sat down again. 'That's why I wanted him to give the thing up. When he was learning he fell over and broke a wing. And then again when he was starting to go up he'd an accident and fell about ten feet or so. That also broke a wing.'

'The same wing?'

'Yes.'

'Which?'

'God, I don't know. The right, I think.'

'Did he get it professionally repaired?'

'No. Ben was forever trying to do things himself. Wasn't he like that when you knew him?'

'I suppose so.' But this was not the case. Ben had always relied on others to do mechanical things for him. Still, perhaps he had changed—he must have, given what she had said about Ben's preparations in the garage.

'So it may well be that Ben made a mistake?' This seemed likely if Ben had taken to do-it-yourself—he might not have been very competent—but he wanted the woman to confirm it.

'I suppose so,' she said slowly. 'At least that's a better scenario than what you were hinting at.'

Jarvis raised an eyebrow.

'You implied that Ben might have been murdered,' she said bluntly.

Jarvis sighed. 'I suppose I did. But one's got to think of every possibility. I'm sorry.'

She spread her hands. 'Go on. You've got a job to do.'

'Do you know of anyone who might have been that ill-disposed to Ben?'

'You said it yourself,' she replied. 'There's a few that might have taken the chance to sideswipe him with a car, but no one that would . . .' She fell silent.

'Had Ben had any arguments with anyone recently?'

She paused a moment in thought before replying. 'Now you come to mention it, there was that French fellow.'

Jarvis waited while she pursued the thought. Then: 'No,' she said. 'That's not likely.'

'Perhaps I should be the judge of that.'

'Well—' she spoke slowly, drawing the memory out little by little—'we did have a big row some months ago with a French associate. It was over a picture he'd sold us. He wanted it back, but we'd sold it on. He said we'd had it on option to show a client and the option had expired. But we hadn't. We'd bought it. Mind you, if what he said was right, we made monkeys of ourselves. He said it was worth five if not six figures.'

'But how did that come into things? Presumably you could tell him who you'd sold it to.' Jarvis finished his drink.

'We did. He didn't let on why he wanted to get in touch. As far as I can remember, he said it was because he'd found another by the same artist that would make a pair. We were going to share the profit on the sale of the second—he promised that, if I recall aright. But in fact when he came over, the painting he brought was nothing like the other, not really. And it turned out that all he was wanting was the address of our client. But our client wouldn't play ball—wouldn't sell back the first picture, I mean. That was when the Frenchman exploded.'

'I see.'

'He was quite violent, in fact. He hit Ben. Hard. Ben had to get a stitch above his eye.'

'Can you give me his name?'

'I expect I could if I looked. Do you really want it?' She glanced in the direction of the rolltop desk, but did not move.

Jarvis spread his hands and nodded. 'Just at present anything's interesting.'

He waited, expecting her to fetch the Filofax that was so clearly visible on the desk, but when she continued to look at him, he carried on. After all, there was nothing to indicate that it served as an address book for the business. 'Was there anything else to indicate this Frenchman carried a grudge?'

'I think so. Ben said he'd had a few abusive phone calls

after that. He used to deal with the French end of things, and said that Maurice—that was his name, I seem to remember . . . Anyway Ben said he was a bad one to get on the wrong side of. In fact, now that I think of it, he hinted that Maurice was mixed up in various things and had got several competitors in Paris—how did he put it?—was it "slowed down"?' She shrugged prettily, then sobered. 'I suppose that means it might have been . . .' She swallowed nervously.

Jarvis waited while she got control of herself once more.

'I don't suppose it does mean much,' he observed. 'But even at that it'd be useful if you could give me the name. Sometime once you get past the immediate few days. They'll be difficult. I suppose you've shut the Gallery meantime?'

'Yes. I couldn't face going in there just now. There were only the two of us. It's not as if there was anyone I could ask to keep it going meantime—no employees, I mean.'

'Will you keep it going?' Jarvis was blunt.

She nodded. 'Yes. There's nothing else. And it'd be an interest, of course.'

'I hate to pry, but has Ben left you all right financially?'

She shook her head slowly. 'Not very well off, but OK, I suppose. There's this house. It's in my name in any case. And there's the business. That must be worth a bit—I haven't really thought.'

'Insurances?'

'There should have been some.' Her tone was flat.

Jarvis raised his eyebrow. 'Should?'

'We argued about all that when he started that damn gliding business. I even got our lawyer to speak to him. Hang-gliding's one of those dangerous sports that they won't pay out for unless you've specially insured for it. It's like going down the Cresta Run, or going up in one of those space things—you know, the one that exploded.'

'And he didn't extend the insurance?'

'No. He was funny that way. He hated that sort of thing. It was with difficulty I got him to insure at all. He was superstitious—hated anything that suggested he might die. Getting him to make a Will was a major operation.'

Jarvis nodded. Ben had had a superstitious streak, now that she mentioned it. He hadn't taken skiing insurance when they'd gone to Chamonix. But then his thought skittered on from that to Pat skiing . . . Then crumpling in the snow, and the cable-car carrying him on and away. His face froze.

'Would you like another drink?' she asked.

'No,' he said quietly, with a slight shake of his head.

'What's wrong?'

He sighed. 'I had an attack of memory. Nothing to do with you or Ben. It was just something you said.'

She looked concerned, but his train of thought had been broken, and he didn't feel like trying to re-establish it. He looked at his watch. 'I'm sorry I've taken up so much time. Perhaps if there's anything more I could get in touch again?'

'Please do.'

He got to his feet.

'Tell you what,' she went on. 'You give me an address, and I'll invite you to the reopening of the Gallery. I am going to have a proper "relaunch". Let folk know I'm back in business, you know.'

'I don't expect to be in Glasgow very much longer.'

'I'm reopening next week. It's like getting back on a horse as soon as possible after a fall. Even if you don't like Ben's painting, you might care to come to a reception?' Her final tone was arch.

'Well, I'm not very sure of my movements. But you could leave a message with Inspector Cohen. He'd get it to me wherever I am.'

'I'll do more than that. I'll invite him too!' She gurgled a laugh.

Jarvis excused himself.

On his way back into Glasgow he went over what had just occurred. He did not know what to make of it. She was different from what he had expected. In some ways she was more upset, in some ways less. He wondered what Lynn Turpin would be like.

A dull pain began in his right side, below the ribs. He

caressed it briefly before digging the antacids out of his pocket. Blast, he thought. It would be just like the thing if all this rushing around about Ben triggered his gut problem once more.

2

Food helped, as it usually did, and Jarvis made his way to Cohen's office.

'What have you got scheduled?' Cohen greeted him.

'Nothing until four-thirty. I'm seeing Turpin's former wife at the Transport Museum.'

'The Transport Museum?' Cohen clearly thought that a most unusual place to conduct an interview.

'The Transport Museum. We knew each other before she married Ben, and I thought it best to meet on neutral ground, as it were. In any case she's got a young son. He can roam about while we talk.'

Jarvis saw Cohen was still puzzled.

'She's a teacher—not free during the day. And when she's off from school, so's the boy.'

Cohen shrugged. 'Oh, well. I suppose you know your business best.'

'Had you anything in mind before then?' Jarvis's tone was mildly interested.

'If you like, we can go out Strathblane way and talk to the secretary of the local hang-gliding club there. I phoned him. He'll be around all afternoon.'

'Have you people talked with him before?'

'Yes.'

'To no effect?'

'Not really. He filled us in a bit on the mechanics of the thing, but that was all. His view was that it was a dreadful accident.'

'Still, I suppose it would be useful for me to have a word too.' Jarvis thought it might be as well to speak to an expert rather than get the information second hand. So Cohen phoned to confirm the appointment and then the two set off.

*

The secretary was an enthusiast. As he responded to Jarvis's initial questions, even Jarvis began to appreciate that soaring free might be exhilarating.

'Tell me,' Jarvis asked, 'what sort of precautions would you take. Is a helmet usual?'

'Of course.'

'What about a parachute—for precisely the case of a collapsing airframe?'

'Some do. Some don't. Ben didn't.'

'I'd have thought it was an elementary precaution.'

'True. But some people think it would make the glider too heavy. The whole thing works because you get more lift from the wing than you and the glider weigh. Ben was a big man. I think that's what decided him against a 'chute.'

'Any other reason?'

'There's also a view that a parachute could impede your controlling the glider. You've got to be free to move back and forth, as well as side to side.'

'So, from what you're saying, there's no requirement to use a parachute.'

'None.'

'So there was never any question of Ben being foolhardy in not having a parachute.' Jarvis was keen to have the matter exactly confirmed.

'No. None at all.'

'Do you use one yourself?'

'Yes. I do. To me it's just an elementary precaution. But not everybody thinks that way.'

'Are there many such accidents? Things that need a 'chute?'

'Not nowadays. There were some accidents when the sport was taking off—if you'll excuse the pun. People didn't understand some of the forces involved. One or two even repaired their gliders with substandard materials. I remember reading about one bloke who used a cord from his window-blind. He didn't survive.' The man shook his head briefly at the foolishness of it. 'But that doesn't happen now. Oh, there are accidents. But not usually because of equipment failure. It's more a case of wrong flying—stalling and such-like. Or collisions.'

'I see. Well, thanks. You've been very helpful.' Jarvis turned to leave, then turned back. 'There is one thing. Had Ben done any work on his glider—repairs or such-like?'

'Not that I know of. But I wouldn't necessarily know about that.'

'Anything there?' asked Cohen as they left. 'He said nothing new to me.'

'I suppose he just confirmed things. It's just that there might have been something. It would have worried me if I hadn't spoken to an expert myself.'

Cohen tossed his head slightly. Clearly he thought Jarvis could have relied on the police files.

3

Jarvis was early for his appointment with Lynn Turpin. She was due at 4.30, but he arrived at 4.10. He wanted time to prepare himself for the encounter. Besides, she had said for them to meet at the seat with the horses. He had to find that.

He had never been in the Kelvin Hall and so was unprepared for the sight of the Transport Museum itself. Carved out of the old Hall, the new museum fitted around the rear and side of the new indoor sports centre. Despite therefore sharing a site, the new museum was large, much more spacious than its predecessor on the south side of the city. Here the trams and railway engines had space to breathe: one could stand back and get a much better impression of them. Immediately inside the door he faced the fire-engines exhibit. To its right were the trams, and the seat that Lynn had mentioned. Her apparently cryptic reference made complete sense. Two dummy horses pulling a tram stood with their heads above a garden seat. He crossed to it and sat.

In front of him a stair led up to two balconies, one to his left above the motor exhibits, the other appearing to stretch the length of the museum above the entrance. He wondered what might be up there. On the left balcony above the motor-cars some sort of glass and wooden structure resembled a small Victorian greenhouse. The other exhibits there were hidden, their backs to the railings. The balcony immediately in front of him showed tantalizing gleams of chromium.

He looked back to the door. A constant stream of visitors was outlined by the light of the entrance. That would not do. He did not want Lynn to approach their meeting with the light behind her and falling on him. The balcony would allow him to see Lynn arrive and let him watch her unobserved. Her demeanour might give him a clue as to how he should approach her and ask the questions he must ask.

On the balcony he found a collection of bicycles and motorcycles, ranging from very old to almost new. At one end, as a separate item, was a three-wheeled 'customized' motorcycle apparently powered by a Volkswagen engine. It looked fun.

Behind the Volkswagen was the Clyde Room. He put his head round the corner and saw the huge glass casefuls of model ships. That would have to wait. He had to see Lynn first.

He looked at his watch. Seven minutes to go. He went to where the greenhouse-like structure had caught his eye. As he reached it the device inside it trembled and then moved. On closer inspection he found that it was working. That pleased him, for it was a Fulton's Orrery. He watched in delight. Then it stopped. He walked round it, marvelling at the fashioning, the intricate cogs, the way each planet on its own arm was interrelated with the others, the use of differentials and eccenters along thread to show the orbits of the principal comets and asteroids Fulton had known about.

Somewhere a time switch closed, and the device began to work again. He watched again, fascinated.

When it stopped he checked his watch. It was past time. He went to the balcony rail. There was no sign of Lynn. He bit his lip. The Lynn he had known would not be late. Of course, that was many years and many experiences ago; yet surely she would remember his own passion for punctuality? But would that bring her if she had learned other habits? Should he go down to the appointed seat? Should he stay up here and wait? Suddenly he was quite uncertain. Suddenly it felt like their first date.

He walked back along the long gallery, past the motor-cycles, glancing down to the main floor. She still had not appeared by the time he had reached the entrance to the Clyde Room. He pursed his lips, then decided that if she wanted to make him wait, he would not play ball. He went into the Clyde Room.

The glorious models lay in their ranks in a room larger than the old Clyde Room in the Art Gallery across the road. He moved down the main aisle, past the sailing ships, the men-o'-war, and then on towards the huge models of the *Hood* on one side and the *Queens* on the other.

In the middle of the aisle just before the *Queens* was a round grey-coloured plush seat, a cone projecting up in its middle making a backrest for the weary. A hunched figure sat on its other side, facing away from him. He hesitated, and then sat down. 'Hallo, Lynn,' he said.

She glanced at him. 'We were early, so I brought Ben up here,' she explained. As if on cue, Ben appeared from between two of the glass cases. 'You carry on,' she said to him. 'I'm talking to Mr Jarvis.'

The boy looked quizzically at them, and then vanished.

'What are you thinking?' asked Jarvis.

'It's been a long time.'

The light from the display cases was pitiless. Looking at her, Jarvis agreed. It had been a long time. She had gone past youth, and her face showed the lines of a demanding life of many disappointments. Her head seemed now to be set a little forward, and her shoulders, which he remembered as fine-boned, were now fleshy. He wondered what she saw.

'I'm sorry we're meeting in these circumstances,' he said. But he realized he was sorry they were meeting at all. He had never tried to get in touch with her after her divorce, nor inquired of mutual friends where she was or what she was doing. Somehow he knew she knew that. And at one time he had thought they might marry!—not that he had ever made any serious moves in that direction. Perhaps that was why Ben had found her so easy to sweep off her feet. But by the time of her divorce there was Pat. Yes: it might have been better never to meet again. Certainly the now mature—even early middle-aged—Lynn, was a savage contrast to the elfin grace of the Lynn of memory. He had prized his memories, not the person.

'You said it was business.'

As she spoke she turned away, once more hunched over, and that triggered another memory.

'Were you up Ben Lomond last Sunday?'

She nodded.

'Why didn't you speak?'

She did not pretend she had not known who had come up behind her on the peak. 'Your being there meant Ben's death wasn't the simple thing it seemed. And I just couldn't take that. Not then. It was bad enough when you confirmed it at the crematorium.'

'And now?'

She turned to look at him. 'It's still difficult.'

'There's no reason for you to think like that,' he said. 'You know it's just routine. It was probably an accident.'

She shook her head. 'No. You're a storm petrel.'

'That's unfair!'

'Think about it.'

'I don't mean you any harm,' he said, but the bleakness of her smile stopped him from saying more on that line.

'I've got to ask you some things,' he said apologetically, putting his hand into his inside pocket and thumbing the recorder it contained. 'Do you mind if I take some notes?' He took some index cards from the pocket, and a pen from his breast-pocket.

'No.' Her face was blank. He did not know if she suspected the recorder's existence.

'Have you had any contact with Ben recently?'

She shook her head. 'All that goes through the lawyers.'

He raised an eyebrow.

'Occasionally there's been a question of school fees—when they go up—things like that.'

'Maintenance?'

'I've never pressed. Only for Ben.' She glanced down the rows of cases to where the boy probably was.

'He paid you no maintenance?'

'There was an agreement. It's fixed to the rate of inflation. It's worked OK.'

'Ben's maintenance or your own?'

'Both. I was talking about mine, actually. Ben's had jumps with schooling and so on.'

'And you never had any trouble?'

'Late payment sometimes, but not trouble. A letter from Mr Stewart always seemed to do the trick.'

'Stewart?'

'My lawyer.'

'So you've not seen Ben at all, recently, and were quite happy with how things were between you?'

She nodded.

'Did he have rights of access? ... I assume you got custody.'

'One day, one a fortnight. We agreed that.'

'He never asked for more?'

'I thought he might as Ben grew older. There's things a father usually wants to do with a son. But no. There was never any word.'

'Like?'

She shrugged. 'I don't know. Going to football matches. Things like that.'

'What about sports?—I mean real sports, not just going along to see things.'

'I heard he was into hang-gliding. I'd not have allowed that.' She was definite.

'How did you hear he was gliding?'

'He started gliding years ago. Not long after the divorce. Real gliding, that is. But the hang-gliding ... I don't know. I just heard it somewhere. It might even have been in the papers. You know what he was like about attracting publicity.'

It was Jarvis's turn to nod. But this was getting nowhere. 'What's happening under the Will? I take it there's a Will.'
'I believe Ben gets a share. The widow gets the rest.'
Jarvis did not ask what Lynn Turpin thought of that, nor if she knew of the bequest to himself.
'We don't know how much Ben's share will be yet. I'm told there's a lot of debt. There won't be much.'
Jarvis pursed his lips, and Lynn read his mind. 'The house is in her name.'
No more was said on that topic. Jarvis knew he could come back to such questions if necessary, but at present there was no need to force or probe. 'There's not much you can tell me, then?'
'I'm afraid not.' She was suddenly still. That immediately worried Jarvis. Years ago it had meant there was something she was concealing from him, something she would not reveal. He had missed something, some key he had not hit, some trigger not pulled, some avenue unexplored. Unexplored? More like undiscovered! Still, it was too late for the present.
He got to his feet, putting the index cards away into his inside pocket and switching off the recorder as he did so. 'I've not seen this place. Do you think Ben'd show me it? How old is he, by the way?'
'Twelve past.' She got to her feet. 'Ben,' she called.
'Mum!' The tone was a mixture of rebuke and disappointment.
'If you've not finished here, how about showing me your favourite models first?' Jarvis asked the youngster as he came towards them.
And, with all the enthusiasm of twelve years, Ben did just that.

'Would you like to come to dinner one evening?' asked Lynn Turpin, as they separated.
Jarvis hesitated. He had wondered if he should invite her out. But that might re-start things. Or worse, it might re-open old wounds without benefit to either of them.

She saw his hesitation. 'It's all right, then,' she said tartly.

He tried to retrieve things. 'No. I was just going over appointments.'

She seemed to believe him. 'Next week?' she asked. 'Monday?'

So it was arranged.

CHAPTER 6

Friday

Morning brought a development. When Jarvis entered Cohen's office about half past eleven, Cohen sifted through the papers on his desk, shoved an envelope across to him, and waited quietly for him to read its contents.

Jarvis raised his eyebrow as he slid the papers back to Cohen. 'Well now,' he said. 'What about that!'

Cohen got up from his desk and went to the window. 'It's appalling to think of,' he said. 'Appalling. The poor bloody fool. He must have done it himself when he was working on the thing.'

Jarvis came and stood beside him. 'A thirty-five-kilo glider. A what—an eighty- or ninety-kilo man? A wire with a breaking strain of one hundred and forty. An updraught or a turn would easily have brought the weight over that.'

They looked down at the passing traffic.

After a moment Jarvis added, 'I wonder what the other tests they're doing are.'

Cohen shook his head. 'We'll hear if it's anything important.' He went back to his desk and sat down.

'Unless,' said Jarvis meditatively.

'Unless what?'

Jarvis shook his head slightly and came back to the other side of Cohen's desk. 'Your people were rather heavy-handed when they talked to Imogen Turpin,' he observed.

'How d'you mean?' replied Cohen, leaning forward with

a frown. A brown file lay in front of him. Jarvis could read the label 'Turpin' on it. It was not very thick.

'Someone asked her whether she and Ben were having marital problems.'

Cohen stared at Jarvis until he felt he had to add something to what he had just said. 'Apparently someone was hinting that they weren't getting on too well in bed.'

Cohen sat back. 'I didn't put it quite like that. It was just that at the time she didn't appear all that upset.'

'Shock? Sometimes people shut down emotionally in the face of something like that.'

Cohen shrugged.

'She certainly was upset yesterday,' Jarvis went on. 'I asked what the police had said, and she quite broke up.'

'I'm sorry to hear that.' Cohen dismissed Jarvis's comment. 'She's cooperating with you, at least. She phoned in an address for you. Somewhere in Paris.' He opened the file and handed over a small sheet from a memo pad. The name Jack Maurice was written on it, with an address in Paris 3. 'Said you'd know what it was about.'

'Thanks.' Jarvis made a note of his own and handed the paper back. Cohen slid it into the file and then tapped the file with his index finger. Jarvis noted that he had been biting his nails. 'Anything else?'

'You asked me to get the reporters checked to see if there was anything said up the mountain that wasn't on the videos.'

'And?'

'There's nothing much. Everyone says Turpin was in good form. One reporter said he had commented on the way up about the mental state of someone trusting himself to a few bits of wire and cloth, and Turpin was quite emphatic about it. According to him these things were as safe as bicycles, if not better, for he checked it out every time he went up—something folk don't do with bikes.'

'So if someone had tampered with the wires, he'd have noticed.'

'Unless he did it himself,' said Cohen easily.

'And the widow says he did replace something himself.'

Cohen nodded. 'Did she say anything about insurance?'

'Didn't you ask her?'

'Of course, but I was wondering what she might have said to you.'

'Why?'

'Just a thought.'

'You tell me why you're asking first.'

Cohen paused. 'I was wondering if there were business difficulties. If it wasn't an accident it might be an insurance plot. But I still think it was a mistake, for all you don't seem to be convinced.'

Jarvis waved a dismissive hand. 'Insurances usually exclude dangerous sports. He'd have had to pay a special premium to have hang-gliding included—or excluded from the exclusion.' He waited, but Cohen said nothing, waiting for him to go on. At length Jarvis pursed his lips. 'For what it's worth, she told me that he had refused to extend his insurance to cover hang-gliding, even though she had pressed him to do so.'

'Hmm. That shows that she was thinking of her future, at least. Sensible girl.'

'How was the Gallery business doing?'

'Probably you know that better than I do. Imogen Turpin clammed up on us, and I've not seen his business accounts. Not yet. If this business does turn nasty I'll have them in a trice. But maybe you can enlighten me—off the record, of course.'

Jarvis allowed an answering wintry smile to cross his face, and, without quite conceding Cohen's thrust, replied, 'According to his accountant, on paper his business wasn't prospering. At least, that's as far as the accounts were concerned, but I got the distinct impression that he felt there were a fair amount of cash transactions that weren't going through the books.'

'I told you I thought something was going on at the Gallery.' Cohen's reply was brisk.

'You were a bit more specific than that. You implied that he was taking a cut from fencing stolen French art, and raised some question whether he might have been involved in some of the drug-running that's been happening on the West Coast.'

'Was I that indiscreet?' Cohen spoke slowly, shaking his head as if stunned by his own indiscretion. He was a ham actor.

'Yes.'

Cohen smiled. 'So where does that get us?' He leaned forward again.

'So you're wondering about suicide? The insurance—if there was one—might tie in with that. And you say a reporter says Ben said he had checked the glider over. If he was intent on suicide for insurance purposes, he'd want no one checking that out.'

'Well, that could be an option.'

Jarvis sat back. 'Now look!' he said. 'Someone committing suicide by hang-glider can do so without arranging for a wire to break.'

'That's true,' Cohen said slowly.

Jarvis had a thought. 'Unless he's wanting to give his heirs a chance to sue the glider manufacturers. But then the manufacturers are going to want to examine the thing themselves.'

'Go on.'

'And that would blow the whole question wide open. But you think, in fact, that it was an accident. That he had misrepaired his hang-glider.'

'My mind is open,' Cohen repeated, turning his head aside to look at the window.

Jarvis smiled. 'Or more accurately, you're sitting on the fence, but you've got your legs over on the "accident" side. You think his Gallery business was doing better in fact than he was disclosing to his accountant—or presumably to the Inland Revenue. So you ask yourself: why should he commit suicide?'

Cohen smiled back.

'So it must be an accident?' Jarvis paused and went on. 'You've not only got your feet over on the accident side, you're starting to get off the fence on that side. You can't see that he would insure himself and then commit suicide.

Well, for what it's worth, I can't see Ben doing the decent thing to get his creditors off the hook either.'

'But you, on the basis of the little you've seen and heard, don't agree the accident theory—that it was a matter of an unintended misrepair.'

'I'm not sure that I don't agree, but I'm not sure that I do agree either.'

'Why?'

'I don't know.' Jarvis got to his feet and walked over to the window. Below, the traffic was jamming up. He turned. 'The Ben I knew wouldn't have taken the risk of messing himself up on a do-it-yourself job. He wasn't terribly competent at that sort of thing, though he was good at using things others said were OK. Repairing his glider with understrength wire just doesn't fit. He'd more likely have got it done by someone.'

'How well did you know him recently? I thought you said you were colleagues way back. Maybe he got bitten by the do-it-yourself bug after your time. Maybe he got overconfident—careless in his old age. Maybe he changed.'

Jarvis turned to the window again.

'So maybe he made a mistake,' continued Cohen, getting up and crossing to the window beside Jarvis. 'After all, how do you tell the strength of a wire? At that gauge you couldn't tell by looking at it.'

'That's a point. Where would he have got it? Presumably he bought it. In that case he'd have relied on the seller giving him the right stuff. I suppose if you're wanting to repair your glider you go into an appropriate shop and buy a length of wire with a breaking strain high enough to do the job.'

'And in that case we could find whoever that was, and if they're selling weak wire for strong that'd be the end of it.' Cohen went back to his desk and sat down. 'I've already got my people working on that. It was an obvious question. We've been round the appropriate places already this morning since that letter came in. There are only two. But no one remembers Turpin buying from them.' His inflection made it clear that Jarvis was barking up a tree that the police had already shown to lack cats.

Jarvis came back to the other side of the desk, ignoring the other's sarcasm. 'Yes. There may be some other supplier you don't know about, but if they're selling understrength wire, I suppose that would pretty well wrap it up. Keep looking. But in the meantime I've got some other matters to consider. Will you let me know how you get on?'

'Surely.' Cohen suddenly hesitated in the face of Jarvis's imperturbability. 'Am I allowed to ask what lines of inquiry you're going to be following?'

'You're allowed to ask,' replied Jarvis with a pleasant smile. 'And I'm not going to tell you anything other than that I'm going for a drive.'

Cohen looked at him. Jarvis wasn't swinging his weight about, and his own irritation evaporated as various options flickered through his mind. 'Doon the watter?' he asked.

Jarvis smiled again.

'More particularly sea lochs?' asked Cohen.

'Now why would I be doing that?' asked Jarvis, his continuing smile encouraging the other to carry on.

'If you're from who I think you are, then that's the most obvious place round here that might be of interest, though I'm damned if submarines have anything to do with art galleries.'

'You shouldn't put your eternal destiny up as a gambling stake. Someone might call in the bet.' Jarvis smiled, then relaxed. It would make no difference for Cohen to know, and it might help things if he felt he was being trusted.

Jarvis crossed to the door. 'You're quite right. I've got someone to see down there. Shall I bring you back some Loch Fyne haddock?'

Cohen nodded, pleased at his deduction, but then swiftly shook his head before his reaction was taken as an acceptance. 'No, thanks. I've got a boxful at home—the wife's got a cousin in the business.'

'Suit yourself.' Jarvis left.

Cohen pencilled himself a note of their conversation. At

its foot he put: 'If not an accident, and not suicide, then . . . M ???' He looked at the door as if Jarvis was still there, closed the file and went down the corridor to tell his deputy to make sure to talk to the Strathblane glider secretary. That way they'd be able to track any unorthodox repair shops he knew of and get this business completed soon.

2

It had been a long time since Jarvis had been along the Clyde. He left Glasgow on the M8, crossed the Kingston Bridge and swept westwards in his steel-grey Volvo estate along the motorway. As he went the day seemed to grow darker, clouds banking up ahead of him, slaty and threatening.

The road bore him swiftly to Greenock. From there it was a short distance to Gourock and the Caledonian Macbrayne ferry for Dunoon. He left his car beside the ferry terminal and on the way across played the tourist, complete with camera. The water was calm, though there was a hushed expectancy. It was going to rain later—that was clear. There might even be a storm.

To his great pleasure, a nuclear submarine was making its way back to its base. They crossed behind it, most of the ferry passengers lining the rails to see the leviathan, although there were a few to whom it was no novelty and who paid no attention. Jarvis noted that even the adults were more interested than fearful, and the few children aboard were delighted. The ferry rocked in the wash. That, far more than the lazy whalelike appearance of the shiny black monster, showed just how large the mighty vessel must be. He took a few photographs.

At Dunoon he walked ashore along the short pier. The air was still. There was no sign of Harvey. He went right, past the parallel jetty and so to the East Bay Promenade. There he made his way to the appointed café and ordered a coffee while he waited.

It was not long before the tall, rangy, almost elegant form of his friend appeared, loping along the sea side of the sea-front, then swerving abruptly, as if homing in—Jarvis thought irreverently—on the café.

They had not met for some years, but Harvey was one with whom such gaps meant nothing. Their rapport was as swift as if they had parted only the day before. Jarvis had a few such friends, and prized them greatly.

'So then, little buddy, what brings you down to this neck of the woods?' Harvey asked as the waitress moved away after bringing him a coffee.

Jarvis smiled at the acknowledgement of the four-inch superiority of his friend. 'Would you believe the innocent pleasure of your company draws me?'

'Nope!'

Jarvis grinned. 'Well, maybe I've offended someone or other and this is my punishment. Some sort of purgation.'

Harvey waved a hand globally, embracing Dunoon and the whole Clyde estuary. 'This might make a good substitute for the Purgatory Dante describes, but I bet the only purgation you've ever had was when they enema-ed you before they ripped out your appendix! Come on. Be serious.'

There was something in the tall man's eyes that told Jarvis that the fun was over.

'Ben Turpin,' he replied quietly. 'You'd have heard of the death. Of course we're investigating.'

'Heard about it? I saw it on the TV—at least the bit they showed.' Harvey drained his coffee and gestured to the waitress for another. 'I thought it might be that, but you never know. There just might have been something else.'

'Should there be?' Jarvis asked innocently. Occasionally his American friend had drawn his attention to things that his own superiors didn't know about. This time he was perturbed to find Harvey smiling at him oddly.

'Sorry, old son. There's been a squeeze from way high up on a couple of things. I trust you—but there's still some suspicion of your bosses' competence.'

Jarvis shrugged. That was the way of things. 'Does that affect the Turpin business too?' he asked.

'Nope. And because I guessed that might be what you were coming down about, I looked over things to see whether we had anything of interest.' He leaned on the table, interleaving his fingers before placing the index fingers together and shaking them gently up and down. Jarvis remembered the gesture. 'The short answer is that we haven't—at least not in my view. There's a comment by one of the guys a year or so ago that he'd been told that the Turpin Gallery was a place to pick up good quality nineteenth, early twentieth minor French painters—Impressionists and later—with no questions asked and satisfactory answers given. But we're not the Internal Revenue Service.'

Jarvis looked puzzled.

The waitress arrived with the extra coffee.

'It's a way of bringing back home some funds without running into taxation questions,' Harvey explained drily. 'Take a picture home as furnishings, and sell it into the art trade. It can be worth a couple of thousand or so—sometimes more. You buy here, and make a nice profit.'

'So how's the Revenue interested?'

'If you do it as a business, it might affect your tax bite.'

'Ah. I see. But is that worth very much?'

'Apparently so. But not enough to worry us. In any event—' he shrugged—'it's mostly the officers, or their wives, that do it.'

'You mean that Turpin was selling the pictures below what he would get if he had exported them to the US in the normal way?'

'Sometimes.'

'I see.' Jarvis played with the spoon. 'Sticking with those pictures, then, to me that means that there was something wrong with them. Either that they weren't whatever you said—was it Impressionists?'

Harvey nodded.

'No, it wasn't,' stated Jarvis. 'You're talking later than that—post-Impressionists, perhaps.'

'I'll take your word for it.'

'The other possibility is that the pictures were genuine antiques, but for some reason he was willing to accept less than fair market value.' Jarvis looked up at his friend who nodded again, his eyes on his interlaced fingers.

'Which is it?'

'I believe some were genuine—maybe most of them. We've never done a check. Maybe Turpin didn't know Stateside prices. Or he might have bought cheap himself and be making enough to make it worthwhile for him. Or both.'

Jarvis sat back and stretched. 'Tell you what I don't understand in all this,' he observed lazily.

'Yes?' His friend had a twinkle in his eye as he looked up, head on one side.

'You seem to have a lot of information on something you yourself said was unimportant.'

Harvey smiled, produced some money, put it beside the empty cups and got to his feet. 'Let's walk,' he said.

Outside, the wind was getting up. Although the town sheltered them from it, Jarvis could see white-tops out on the Clyde. They strolled along the front, past the ferry pier and the mound capped by the inevitable war memorial and so round into the West Bay. There they were exposed to the westerly wind, and Jarvis hunched himself against the chill air. Harvey, on the contrary, straightened in the freshening breeze and Jarvis remembered his friend was prone to wax eloquent about his Maine fisherman forebears. But this was not the time for that sort of reminiscence.

'You're right, of course,' said Harvey. 'I got the info about the pictures from another file. Guess which?'

Jarvis thought quickly. It came to him. 'Not drugs?' he questioned bleakly. There had been Cohen's comment, and there had been recent newspaper accounts of Customs seizures on the West Coast up near Oban.

Harvey nodded. 'Drugs is a major matter of concern with us round here,' he observed. 'There was an awful fuss some years back about marijuana being used on the bases. You maybe remember. Hell! It scared me. If someone on watch was high on substances, we might be into World War III . . .' He whistled expressively. 'Or at least that was the point then. Hopefully we've got some way back from that, with what's going on over there.' He waved a hand in a general easterly direction.

Jarvis sighed. 'So Ben crops up in a drugs file.' His shoulders drooped. He was more than disappointed.

'Hold up, little buddy. We've got nothing explicit. When I indexed the name, that's where the computer told me to look. All that was there was a suspicion, nothing more. And when someone had done some checking out of the suspicion, he came up with the pictures question. That might be indicative of criminality, but there was nothing on drugs. I assure you about that. There were a few others involved in drugs, but not your Ben.'

'Even so, it's something else for me to think about.' Jarvis walked a few paces, then stopped and looked out across the water. The clouds were darkening. 'Look. How would you react to this script? Ben gets involved with the drug-ferrying into the West Coast of Scotland. For some reason something goes wrong. His "friends" arrange an accident, either by way of retribution, or because he scares them for some reason.'

Harvey screwed his face up. He didn't think much of that idea.

Jarvis waved a hand and pressed on. 'Alternatively, Ben wants to get into the drugs scene, but . . . ?' He shrugged expressively.

'That's an awful lot of bush to grow out of the little bit of dirt I just gave you,' replied Harvey equally solemnly.

'But either way there's no question of any security involvement. To be blunt: you folk don't think he was involved in any way in anything that's going on round or into your bases?'

'That's right. The only question that his name came up in was the drugs one. How it came up, I don't know. I might be able to run that down, but we weren't seeking him actively. If he'd been into espionage we'd have been much more interested.'

'You've involved the local police in this?' Jarvis appeared to change the subject.

'Sure,' replied Harvey in a tone that negatived the statement.

'Well, thanks for that! You've given me a couple of things to think about. But I'm glad that Ben wasn't into drugs. That wouldn't be the Ben I knew.'

'Me neither. But then people change, especially when they get a bit older and see the rewards of life going undeservedly elsewhere.'

'Don't be cynical. It doesn't suit you.'

'I'm merely saying what you're thinking, even though you're being polite. Your Ben was after money and wasn't all that scrupulous about giving value for it.'

By common consent they turned and made their way back along the sea-front and round the bluff with the war memorial on it, walking in silence, each wrapped in his own thoughts.

'No,' said Jarvis at last, stopping as they came to the end of the pier and looking out over the muddy greyness of the water and the gathered clouds. 'No. It's simpler than that. Ben could have turned to drugs—that's where the money is. You know that deep down, and I know that deep down. All your file shows is that there's no evidence, and that the little checking your people did showed there was no evidence. And I note you didn't tell me what date your information was.'

Harvey pursed his lips. 'That's true. The file comment is a couple of years back.'

'The accident was a week ago,' Jarvis observed bleakly.

'I'll tell you this at least,' said Harvey slowly. 'I saw some of the pictures that were going through on the deal. They were nice. Country scenes mostly, cows, children playing. Things like that. Tempting.' He grinned.

Jarvis looked at him. 'How much did he charge?' he asked. Harvey's smile grew. 'I paid him ten thousand dollars for four,' he said. 'They're real nice.'

3

The swell was rising, and a drizzle started before the ferry got back to Gourock, masking the hills to the north in veils of mistiness. He had forgotten what that fine Clyde rain could be like, and ran to his car as it started to make inroads. It had grown gloomy enough for him to put on his headlights as he swung back on to the M8 for the return to Glasgow.

He powered along the road, enjoying the feeling of the drive. The contrast of gloom and power—some part of his mind was being satisfied: another was clicking off what Harvey had said, comparing what he already knew.

Back at his accommodation he switched on the TV. *Don Giovanni* was scheduled later on the Music Channel, so, after a bath, that took his mind more or less off business for the rest of the evening.

However, as he fully expected, his subconscious did not go off duty. About half past eleven therefore he settled himself comfortably with a brandy and an A4 notepad and began quietly and gently to skim over what he knew and what he had heard. Where were the patches of ignorance? *Ex hypothesi*, he could not know where he was truly ignorant, but from past experience by laying things out in some sort of pattern on paper he could occasionally see where he was partially ignorant. By working on those areas truth could often be arrived at. Sometimes the gaps, the areas of true ignorance, could be isolated and perceived as it were in reverse colouration, and he could begin to work out what might fill those blanks.

So it proved in this instance. After some forty minutes he had two pages of notes, and a single page with names, dates and interlinking lines and arrows arranged on it.

He sat and looked at that page for a minute or so. Over to one side was the word 'Drugs', with a large question-mark after it. Below it was another—'Paris' with a smaller question-mark.

'Why not?' he asked himself and went to the phone.

Some minutes later, content, he went to bed happy that his subconscious seemed to have some method in its madness. London had traced the names in the book in Turpin's desk. One, Maurice, had the address and phone number that Imogen Turpin had supplied. Jarvis smiled quietly. Computer searching of files saved such long and otherwise arduous labour and made it possible easily to answer what might otherwise be thought of as wild questions.

CHAPTER 7

Saturday

First thing next morning Jarvis phoned London. He knew Appleby's habits, and he was not wrong. Appleby was in, but there was no news from that end.

'Well,' said Jarvis, 'there is something I want you to be ready to do.'

'Yes?' The voice was noncommittal.

'I may want you to back up a request that'll be going in to Customs and Excise up here.'

'Yes?' The voice sounded more interested.

'There might be some connection between Ben Turpin and drug-running. Coming in through some of those beaches on the West Coast—you know—north of Oban, or anywhere up that whole coast.'

'There has been some activity there,' said the voice slowly. 'I can't believe that there would be a connection with Ben.'

'To be blunt, neither can I,' replied Jarvis. 'It's just something else that needs to be eliminated. We'll ask in the usual way, but I'm not sure whether a request for cooperation will produce fast enough action. I want you to expedite it if necessary.'

'I see.' The voice paused, then spoke briskly. 'All right. I'll see to it if you need the help. But I'll wait for your call. Better to let things proceed as naturally as possible.'

'That's true. And it reminds me of something else. Cohen, the man in charge of the Turpin business, was a bit frosty at first. Whoever was in here last on this kind of affair muddied the waters. They're not too keen on people being dropped in on them.'

'Quite right too. You'd not like someone coming in on a matter that you thought was yours. They're the same.'

'But there are ways of coming in that work and ways that don't. Whoever was here last messed things up.'

'I think we had noted that.'

Jarvis knew that tone of voice, and let the matter drop.

'I like this,' he said cheerfully as he came in and waved his hand at the general mess in Cohen's room. 'Makes me feel at home. D'you ever lose things, though? I do.'

'Only if someone stirs the pile,' said Cohen grumpily. 'What can I do for you? You'll not have come in for nothing, I presume.'

Jarvis made a mental note—Cohen: not good in the morning—but smiled pleasantly. 'What's ado?' he asked. 'You don't seem all that happy with the world. Or is it just me?'

Cohen sighed, then a wintry smile passed over his face. 'I'm sorry,' he said. 'Just sometimes things pile up.'

'I know all about that. Who doesn't nowadays? Audit control. Quality monitoring. You name it. I spend too much time filling in forms to satisfy people who couldn't do my job that I am doing it properly!' He spoke feelingly.

Cohen snorted. 'So it's got into the cloisters?'

'It's got into the cloisters!' agreed Jarvis. 'Any tips on how to get it out?'

'Selective assassination,' suggested Cohen. 'Still, I have got a heap of work to do, and I'd be grateful if you didn't add to it by taking me up on what I just said.'

'Tell you what,' replied Jarvis. 'I'll do it off your patch. In any case I really came in to say I've got to go north. Perhaps something'll turn up while I'm away?'

'Lucky you. I wish I could get away for a couple of days. OK. We'll carry on, and I'll see you—when? Tomorrow? Couple of days?'

'When I appear,' replied Jarvis easily, then corrected himself. 'No. I'll be back down on Monday. I've got an appointment that evening. But while I remember, there is something else. Would you get Customs and Excise to tell you if they had any contact—suspicion or whatever—with Ben. I know you people deal with drugs once they're in the country, but they cover the entry into the country, don't they?'

'Humph! You are casting your net wide, aren't you? Or is this the result of your trip yesterday?'

Jarvis raised an eyebrow—after all, Cohen himself had said something about drugs—but Cohen did not notice. He had immediately gone back to his desk, picked up his phone and was turning the leaves of an office telephone directory.

2

Jarvis drove back to Greyhavens. Before going home he went into his office. The letter from Turpin's solicitor was waiting for him, and he pocketed it. There were also a few matters of business to attend to. This he did and then stopped at the corner shop for milk and a frozen pizza.

A few letters lay on the mat behind his door. He threw them all into his favourite chair in the living-room, put on the gas-log fire and went to the kitchen. He put the pizza in the oven. While waiting for the kettle to boil he guiltily watered the plants on the kitchen window sill. The cacti excepted, they were looking sorry for themselves, and the Busy Lizzie had slumped in despair.

He took milk, a mug and the larger of his two teapots through to the living-room, put them on the fireplace surround, and settled himself, the letters easily to hand.

Quickly he sifted them into personal and junk mail, slit each envelope and, contrary to his usual custom, read the personal ones first. There were two letters from friends abroad, a 'Final Warning' for the telephone bill that he had paid before going down to Glasgow, and a bank statement. This he put aside to reconcile with his cheque-book later.

The solicitor's letter was formal, but now he had seen the man himself he could imagine him dictating it. It contained the relevant quotation from Ben's will. He had been left the picture *Icarus Falling*. Ben explained that the bequest was made 'in the hope that he [Jarvis] will study and appreciate it, since I painted it myself—which will doubtless surprise him, and may lead him to value it more highly than hitherto.'

Jarvis dropped the letter to the floor and poured himself a mug of tea. What had possessed Ben to make such a bequest? Come to that, why had he made a will in the last year, for the legacy was obviously triggered by the events at the opening of the Gallery? That led to other questions. Was it a new will, or was it a revision of an old will? If the latter, there might be interesting discrepancies between the new and the one it replaced. Still, all that could be found out if necessary. In the meantime he let his mind wander where it would, remembering this and that of their time together.

The mug empty, Jarvis laid it aside and turned to the junk mail, consigning each item swiftly to a waste-paper bucket. This last was a pride and joy. It purported to be a large tin of Heinz Beans, one suitable for hotel catering, and he had found its capacity just about right for a week's mail.

The third last piece of junk mail was from an insurance company. He sighed as he shook out the contents. His name was on some mailing list or other that had recently been sold into the mushrooming financial market, and there had been many solicitations for business. Yet another invitation from an insurance company to take out unnecessary insurance? He made to tear up the envelope with its contents, then noticed that the envelope was not of the usual form. It did not have the 'give-away' plastic window for the address.

The papers were a letter, an extract from an insurance policy with the company, and a claim form. That was the way they came out of the envelope: he read them in inverse order.

The form invited him to claim the sum of £30,000 from the Crowninshield Insurance Company.

Jarvis was disappointed with himself. He had succumbed to a clever twist on the usual junk mail format. It was another invitation to a share in a Prize Draw for 'new investors'. He dropped the form to the floor beside his chair with a sigh. Sometimes he did fill up such things, provided that entry to the 'Prize Draw' was free, carried no obligation, and had a postage-paid envelope—not that he'd ever won anything.

He checked. This one did not have the postage-paid envelope.

Ah well, that was that. But it might be interesting to see what the advertising executives had dreamed up this time. After all, they had got him not to throw the papers away immediately. He looked at the extract policy to see what the conditions for the Draw were. Not very clever, to use a dummy policy as part of the ploy. Few would plough through such verbiage. The advertisers must be getting desperate! Well, he thought, let's see how badly this is written.

He read the extract policy with growing bewilderment and then re-read it with shock. This was no word-processed insert to a printed form. The £30,000 was payable to him 'in trust to be expended on such charitable and benevolent purposes as he [might] choose, including the relief of the educational needs of orphans'. The money was payable on the death by accident of Bernard Turpin, Art Dealer in Glasgow.

The accompanying letter explained. Ben Turpin had arranged a general accident policy some five months earlier, to run for a period of six months and covering all risks. Although normally excluded from such policies, hang-gliding had been specifically endorsed as a covered risk, and Ben had paid the necessary increased premium. The letter went on:

> The subscriber [a senior official of the company] acted personally in the arranging of this insurance and I am deeply distressed at the death of Mr Turpin, not of course because of the possible financial implications for the Company, but because I found him an interesting man.

He was therefore enclosing an appropriate claim form, though he did:

> find it necessary to add that of course payment [would] be deferred until the suitable conclusion of police inquiries into the death, and you will understand that, were it to be established that Mr Turpin died by his own deliberate action, no monies would be due on the policy.

Lastly, the writer explained lest Jarvis did not know the legal position that money paid under such a discretionary trust was not part of Ben's estate for tax or inheritance purposes, and it was up to him whether he disclosed its existence to anyone. The writer presumed that, as was normal in such cases, Turpin had left with Jarvis a request (though not an instruction) as to the use of the monies.

Jarvis re-read the papers, poured himself another mug of tea and sipped it, gazing into the gold and blue flames playing round the imitation wood-logs. First the picture, and now this! His mind went back to the opening of the Gallery a year before, and to Turpin's comments about his own fooling with insurances. Could it be that as Ben had plummeted out of the sky, his last thought had been of the jokes he had arranged to play on Jarvis?

The pizza was burnt.

CHAPTER 8

Monday

Cohen's office looked as though it had been stirred.

'Some mail for you,' grunted Cohen and rummaged about on his desk. Eventually he unearthed an envelope from a pile of papers and handed it over.

'I bet I know what's in it,' he remarked.

'Go on then,' responded Jarvis, picking up a letter-opener on the desk, but waiting for an answer before using it. Cohen put his index fingers against the sides of his forehead and mimed concentration. Then: 'It's an invitation to the reopening of the Turpin Gallery,' he said, paused, then continued triumphantly. 'Tomorrow night.'

'Ah,' Jarvis responded as he cut into the envelope. 'She said she'd send you one too.'

Cohen let his shoulders slump in a picture of disappointment. 'How'm I going to get any credit for brilliant feats of deduction if folk like you blow the gaff on me?' he inquired plaintively.

Then, obviously, the time for joking was over. He crossed to the window and stared out at the traffic and the passers-by. 'I dare say those folk out there have as clear an idea as I do about Turpin. What about yourself?'

Jarvis lowered his head. Should he tell Cohen about the insurance policy now? Not yet, he decided swiftly. The personal interest he now had in the matter might be misconstrued. Besides, he hadn't told Appleby that morning—why should he now tell Cohen, whom he knew far less well?

He raised his eyes to find Cohen staring at him. 'Sorry. What did you say?' he asked.

'I was wondering if you'd had any more information that might help us. Help tie the thing up. Finish it,' Cohen concluded emphatically.

'You're suddenly very keen to be done.'

'Well—' Cohen gestured widely—'I reckon it's just like we thought at the beginning.'

'We?'

'The bosses up here. They think it's an accidental job. Like I said, he repaired his glider thing with the wrong sort of wire. Went up Ben Lomond. And ping!' He flicked open his fingers. 'There's nothing else to go on. No real cause for suspicion of anyone other than your late and careless friend.'

He went back to the desk and put his hands flat on the table. 'And there's this too. I thought of telling you earlier, but . . .' He shrugged. 'Since I've not been able to report any real progress to my boss, he's minded to close the file and let the Fiscals carry on with their Fatal Accident.'

'Even if I say no?' Jarvis was quiet.

'Reckon so. At least, they'll go over your head to see if they can clear it off. The thing's too mysterious—I mean, what precisely *your* interest is—and the bosses here don't see any point in spinning things out. They think I should be spending my time—and others' time as well—on more productive investigations.' Cohen delivered the last phrase ponderously, bringing vividly to life a senior officer.

'Value for money?' replied Jarvis with a smile. Then he asked, 'How many have you working on this now?'

Cohen sighed. 'Two full time getting hold of all the possible glider repairers by phone.' He caught Jarvis's surprise and explained. 'We're pursuing inquiries all over the country about that. But after that it'll only be one element among everything else that's going on in the world of crime. And if there's a clearer case comes up, or something major . . .' He spread expressive hands.

Jarvis nodded. 'Well, I can see the point. Let's leave it a day or so, if you can.'

'Till the Customs boys have reported?'

With that they separated.

2

Misjudging the time needed to get there, Jarvis was early for his dinner at Lynn Turpin's. He drove past the end of her street and parked to wait until the appointed time. As the car drew to a halt a group of youngsters went past to stand at the nearby bus stop. As he switched off the engine, he realized that young Ben Turpin was among them, and that he had recognized Jarvis. But before Jarvis could decide what, if anything, to do the bus came round the corner and the boys clattered their way aboard.

Jarvis sat a few minutes longer, feeling a blush subside. He was angry with himself. He was angry both for the blush and also for being seen by Lynn's Ben. From somewhere out of his past there crept the young man who had taken weeks to summon the courage to invite Lynn Redpath out in the first place. Feeling once more gauche and more than a little confused, he picked up the large box of chocolates he had settled on as a suitable offering and turned it over in his hands. Should it have been flowers? A bottle of wine? It was too late now.

He drove round the block to Lynn's flat.

She was shy too. As she opened the door he noticed her colour was high, and her voice a little breathless as she thanked him for the chocolates and said that Ben had gone out with his friends—she thought probably to see one of the new releases.

Her slight confusion steadied him. It was like exams, he thought irrelevantly. Throughout his career he had always been scared before examinations, but, when surrounded by others who were obviously nervous as well, his own apprehension had been buried by the interest of observing theirs and the various strategies this one and that adopted to cope with the stress. One, usually taciturn, would become garrulous. Another would make frequent visits to the lavatory. Some bit nails. Many smoked. A few went unnaturally silent.

Lynn chattered.

The flat was not spacious, but adequate. On two floors, it had a kitchen, lounge and dining-room, with, presumably, bedrooms upstairs. She took him into the lounge. To the right of the fireplace in which a small fire burned was the part of the room—it might have begun as a corner—where Ben made his models. There were piles of boy's junk on and around a battered kitchen table with model planes in various stages of assembly and disassembly. One or two swung on thread from the ceiling. As Jarvis crossed over to inspect, Lynn spoke.

'You'll need to excuse the mess. I let Ben have that bit. He hasn't got much room upstairs, and he says he needs to be able to let things lie without tidying up every time.'

'He's pretty good,' replied Jarvis, picking up a Mustang and admiring it. In fact Jarvis was being polite. There were ample evidences of haste in the construction, and, without looking at the plans, Jarvis thought the wingflaps had been transposed and fitted upside down.

'Give me a minute,' said Lynn. 'It's almost ready. Have a seat. Help yourself. There's sherry or whisky over there.' She left quickly.

Jarvis wandered around the room. A bookcase in one corner was filled with Georgette Heyers, Helen MacInnes, Agatha Christie, Ngaio Marsh and similar writers. No 'modern' writers at all, he observed. A watercolour over the mantelpiece next took his attention. It was of a wind-swept bay with spray breaking over rocks at the corner. It was competent. He peered at the signature and made out 'L.R., Arran 1987'.

He turned as Lynn Turpin came back in. 'Yours?' he asked.

She nodded.

'I like it.'

She came over and stood near him, looking at the picture. 'It's not bad. Not quite right, but I think I know what's wrong.'

'I didn't know you painted.'

'I used to when I was a teenager.' She smiled, taking years off her face. 'Some years ago I got the notion to start again.' She looked down at her hands. Small, practical hands with square-cut nails. 'It was good to find I could still do it.' She flexed her fingers.

'Have you any more?'

She put her head on one side. 'Maybe. I mean there are more, but I'm not sure I want to show . . .' Her voice trailed off and he was left wondering whether she didn't want to show them, or didn't want to show him. He could believe either. 'Come on. It's on the table.'

During the meal they talked warily. Once upon a time they had been close. Now the ghosts of Ben and Pat sat with them as they carefully skirted some topics and found in others that a rapport still existed between them. But Jarvis was uneasy. He wasn't sure what he was getting himself into—should he have come?

They returned to the lounge. Jarvis stretched himself in a chair before the fire, then pulled himself up by his elbows and stared into the flames. It reminded him of another occasion—the night they had quarrelled and Ben, coming into the restaurant just at that point, had taken Lynn home. They had been sitting beside an open fire, he gazing into it. He hadn't noticed Ben's approach until Lynn had stood up. 'Here's Ben,' she had said. Then, imperiously, 'Ben. Take me home.' That had been the beginning of the end for them. The next day he had invited a newly arrived assistant to dinner, and by ill-chance they had gone to the same eatery that Ben had selected to take Lynn to. And now for the life of him Jarvis could not remember what he and Lynn had quarrelled about.

'Odd, isn't it? Who'd have thought we'd be sitting here together these years on.'

'I know.' Her voice was quiet, her hands folded in her lap.

He nodded. 'And who'd have thought so much would have happened to us both.'

They sat in silence for a few moments, a silence that threatened to become companionable, then she asked a question.

'What did happen to Pat? It was in the newspapers, but there were all sorts of other rumours.'

He sighed. 'Well, at least they got the location right. It was on the Glacier du Géant, south of Chamonix.' He leaned forward, picked up the poker and prodded at the coals while he spoke quietly. 'But that was all they got right. I was up there picking some film up from a . . . a friend.' He smiled bleakly. 'He went down the other side into Italy from Helbronner. I came back on the cable car. But Pat was down on the glacier. I had asked her to go down there as a routine decoy.' He twisted the end of the poker into a crack in a lump of coal. It split slowly.

'The material was more important than I had realized,' he went on. 'And they had tracked it, probably because it was important. The decoy idea worked too well. They shot her. I was in the cable car above her about a hundred yards away.'

'With the film?'

He nodded.

'Who's "they"?' she asked.

He stared into the fire, unseeing.

The flames crackled.

'I'm sorry,' she said in a small voice. He ignored it.

After a couple of minutes she got to her feet. 'I'll let you see those pictures,' she said in a suddenly practical tone of voice.

He wondered as she left. He hadn't meant to speak, but somehow he had. And her reaction to the story had been odd. Was she shocked? Sympathetic? It was part of the consequences of their break-up. If they hadn't quarrelled, if she had not gone off with Ben, would Pat be alive now? He mused, and then moved on. In the real now, what was going to happen?

He gazed at the flickering fire. 'Salamander. Salamander come to me,' he whispered. 'Is this the future or the past?'

A coal fell with a faint whuff. He smiled at his own silliness, and then shook his head gently. This was the past. For the first time he had told someone other than George Appleby what had happened to Pat, and of all people he had told Lynn! But, he realized, he felt nothing other than relief that he had told someone. And he recognized the feeling. He remembered with some shame that when Ben had gone off with Lynn, his main feeling had been a similar one of relief. Some anger; some pique; yes. But fundamentally he had been relieved. It was the same again. Her closing the matter down by turning to the pictures was typical—a cold, practical streak he had never cared for.

He chuckled and, leaning over, picked up the poker to stir the fire.

'Something funny?' Her voice had an edge to it, her eyes questioning. She was carrying several framed pictures.

He put the poker down and got to his feet. Something inside him had settled. That callow boy had gone back wherever he had come from, though he was now faced with the problem of how to ensure that she didn't think there was something more than old friendship in their reunion. 'Mafeking's relieved,' he said.

She propped the pictures against the table with Ben's models on it. 'That was always one of your most irritating habits,' she said sharply.

He raised an eyebrow.

'And that was one of the others!'

He looked his question.

'You would always say things that no one could follow, and if anyone commented, you'd flick that eyebrow.' She came near to stamping her foot.

'Sorry,' he said meekly. 'Let's see them, then.' He came towards the pile of pictures.

There were four. One after the other she stood them against the back of the settee and one of the easy chairs.

'There's more.' She left the room.

The pictures were all landscapes, competent watercolours done with perhaps a little too much paint so that the paper was filled with blocks of colour rather than the shading that hallmarks a good watercolourist. Watercolours need to show the underlying white of the paper to gain the luminosity which the best contain.

She came back with a few more unframed but mounted pictures, and laid them out in silence.

'They're good,' he said. 'I wish I could paint like that. I was second bottom in Art at school until the boy below me left. We had great fun, and the master put up with us. But I could never get the hang of it.' He looked from one to another, and was generous. 'You've got a gift.'

'They are improving,' she allowed. Last winter I went to evening classes, and that has helped a lot. I'm going to sign up again this autumn.'

'I like that one particularly,' he said, pointing.

'*Goat Fell*,' she said. 'Wait. I've got others. You might like one of those better.' She disappeared again.

When she came back she was carrying several sheets of paper block.

'There. And there's more.' She handed them to him, and

went out again. Laying the pictures on Ben's table, he turned them over. They were good.

Then it seemed as if a cold trowel scooped out his guts, but he forced himself to conceal it. Before him was an evening view, the gold of the setting sun on the mountain contrasting with the purple shadows of the lower slopes. He turned on, putting one picture on top of the other as he went.

She came back with some more which she put to the side of the ones he was looking at.

'You've done all these this year?' he asked as he turned to the new pile.

She was attending to the fire. 'Yes. These are the latest.'

'I think *Goat Fell* is best,' he said, going back to the framed pictures.

'I'd like you to have it.'

He looked at her and she looked at him, then she sighed, and her shoulders drooped a little.

The moment was come. And The Moment was gone. She had accepted that, and with relief he recognized that he was not going to have to disengage himself from her expectations. That would make the next few minutes easier.

'Let's be honest,' she said. 'I did have some hopes we might have something still to rekindle, but it's as plain as a pikestaff we don't. I don't know what's wrong. Whether it's my history, Pat, or whatever you've been doing these years. But I'm not going to fight it. It just might be Ben. But we can still be friends, and I'd like you to have this—I'd like to know you've got something of mine on your wall.' She spoke with a transparently false lightness.

He looked at the picture again. 'That's the nicest dismissal I've ever had,' he said slowly, with what might have been a smile. But there was a coldness deep down behind his eyes.

She saw it and asked. 'What's wrong?'

'I'm interested in this one as well,' he said, pulling one from the pile of unframed pictures.

'I forgot about that one.' Her voice dropped thinly into the silence.

He tapped the picture with a fingernail. Then he leaned forward, inspecting the picture more closely. It was signed: 'L. Redpath. September 1990.'

'Before or afterwards?' he said heavily.

'Before. Two days before. It's from the pier.'

'Can I take it too? Please?'

She nodded.

'Would you mind naming it?'

She fetched a pen, wrote, picked the painting up and gave it to Jarvis.

He looked into her eyes as she handed it over, but she turned away to the fire.

The picture was now named as he had recognized it. *'Ben Lomond from the Pier, Rowardennan.'*

If the dating was right, Lynn had been there just two days before the accident. But was she accurate? Or had she been there the night when the glider was left unattended on the mountainside? The painting was clearly an evening view.

Suddenly memory superimposed the shape of her in the Clyde Room in the Museum of Transport, and the shape of the hunched person at the summit of Ben Lomond. And now this picture. A resentment born of suspicion welled up.

'Why didn't you say something?' he asked fiercely.

She did not pretend not to follow his thought. 'That damned whistling of yours!' She turned, flaring. 'I recognized you immediately you started. But "*By yon bonnie braes*"! Only you could have been that crass. There was no way I could have spoken to you then. You're lucky I didn't go for you with a rock!'

'I'm sorry.' He was sorry. But then how was he to know? And what better to whistle when one has just conquered the ancient Ben? And did that help his lurking question? He was not sure he wanted to know. 'Why were you there?'

'I had to go,' she said solemnly, and he did not press the matter.

But what was he left with? There was the problem of Ben's insurance policy, and of his death. There was the evidence of the picture. Why had Lynn gone to the scene of Ben's death so soon after—or even at all. The outworking of guilt? Was it guilt for a spoiled life? Or was it more direct guilt for the death?'

He sensed that he would have to leave these questions for the moment, yet he could not just depart on such a note. So he sat down, picked up the poker once more and prodded the fire. 'How's Ben doing at school? Where have you got him?'

She named a private school nearby. 'He got in there a year ago. Ben arranged it and pays—paid the fees. I'm not sure what'll happen now. Perhaps he'll be able to get a scholarship. He is very bright.' She sat down opposite and looked into the fire, her hands in her lap.

'Is it very difficult?'

'Ends meet, but that's about all.'

'You've no claim on the estate?'

'No. Young Ben would have his legal rights, but they say the actual estate will be very small. Ben had mortgaged a good deal, and the house is hers.'

Jarvis thought. Would she have known anything about the insurance? There was only one thing to do. Ask. So he did. 'It seems silly that Ben should have indulged in such dangerous sports but taken no steps to insure himself against accident.'

'Just like him.' Her tone was bleak. 'I doubt it would occur to him that he'd others to think of. He'd not have thought of Ben, and I'm of no account now. But I suppose the new wife might have tried.'

'I don't think she succeeded in making him sensible,' he replied, misleadingly.

'What did happen?' She stared at him, willing him to answer.

'A wire broke.'

'But those things don't break.'

'There are other cases of it happening.'

'But not cases where people like you come down to check things out.' Her tone was definite as she turned her gaze back to the fire. There was a moment's silence that seemed to stretch and then she broke it by busying herself with the coal-scuttle.

'I'm surprised you use an open fire.'

'I suppose central heating or gas would make more sense, but I've always liked an open fire.'

'I remember you saying that you liked flame when you used to make those glass ornaments.' He looked around for some but there were none.

'I gave that up when Ben was small,' she said. 'It seemed too dangerous to have a gas cylinder around, or even the mains variety, with a young child. He might be tempted.'

'And there's none of your work either?'

Her shoulders slumped a little. 'When we were moving when things got too bad with Ben, the box got dropped. At least, that's what Ben said, though I have my suspicions.' She pursed her lips.

'And you've never thought of starting again?'

'Oh, I've thought about it. But you don't realize what it is to be a single parent with a full working day to get through and then to come back to a youngster, and a house to run. There's just not been time.'

'Don't put it off too long.' Jarvis got to his feet and went over to the table, moving the paintings to look again at the model planes. 'Ben seems to have inherited your talent.'

'A little. But he's still careless. He wants to see it finished as soon as it's out of the box. I prefer to enjoy doing it before seeing it finished. The planning and the execution, that's half the pleasure.'

Jarvis turned at the comment, and found her as animated by recollection as she had been with her glass-work hobbies all those years in the past. He commented about Fred, another friend who had also worked in glass, and they began to reminisce about other mutual friends from the past. But the words 'planning and execution' kept running round his mind so that he was relieved when Ben arrived home.

Ben was boyishly incoherent: the picture had been 'cool', but not as good as the first in the series, and could he go and see the film that was on next week?

His mother rumpled his hair.

CHAPTER 9

Tuesday

Jarvis arrived late that evening at the Turpin Gallery. It was an effort of will that he arrived at all. Twice on his way from parking the car he contemplated turning on his heel. He found himself unwilling to face the memories of the opening of the previous year and all that had happened since. But for all Ben's faults, and for all that he had stolen (perhaps) Lynn from him, Ben had been a friend. He ought to go. But then, he thought, at least if he were late he might avoid some of the duties of 'light conversation' that he knew he would find difficult. He slowed and did some window-gazing.

When he eventually arrived the Gallery was already quite full. As he entered he saw Cohen over in a corner jerk his head in acknowledgement of his presence. Jarvis collared a sherry from a passing tray, and, now determined to be dutiful, went to the nearest group. They were discussing the death, so he moved onwards.

The second group contained Tessa, Imogen Turpin's sister. She was stunningly dressed in aquamarine which clashed badly with the purplish-red of the wall behind her, but she seemed neither to notice nor care. She smiled at Jarvis as he came to stand near, her eyes narrowing slightly as she did so. She had just disengaged herself from the man she was listening to when Imogen appeared and took Jarvis by the arm, drawing him to one side.

'I'm so glad you could come,' she said.

'It's a good turn-out,' Jarvis responded, waving his glass gently at the assembled bodies.

'I wanted to have a word with you,' she went on, guiding him towards the back of the Gallery. Once past the waist, Jarvis found that there were fewer people. Where *Icarus* had hung was filled with several paintings of fields and cows.

She saw him register the change. 'That's what I wanted to speak about. We've taken *Icarus* down and I want to know whether you want us to dispatch it to you, or whether you want to take it home yourself.'

'I've been thinking about that. I think you should keep it,' he said. 'If I refuse the legacy there'd be no difficulty, provided you're the residuary legatee.'

'So technical!' she said softly. 'But there's no question about it. I have other of his paintings. Ben wanted you to have *Icarus*. And I'd prefer not to have it around. You understand, don't you?' She looked anxiously at him.

Of course he did! What widow whose husband had plummeted out of the sky would want a picture like that on her walls, even if her husband had painted it? He had to retrieve his crassness. 'I suppose I do. Where is it? I've forgotten exactly how big it is. Maybe it'd fit in the car.'

'It's in the glory hole,' she said. 'Just a minute.' She went to the desk that Jarvis had examined and brought out a key. Opening the door in the false wall that formed the waist, she motioned Jarvis to precede her.

'Now, now Imogen. No time for that. Not just now.' The sally came from a young man in a nearby group. The group laughed. She ignored it.

'There's a light on the left,' she said, coming in behind Jarvis, and leaving the door open behind her. 'That's it,' she said, pointing to a frame that was turned against the wall. It looked to Jarvis to be about six feet on its long edge and perhaps four deep, perhaps a bit more.

'I think I can manage that,' he said after a moment. He turned, bumping into her. She smiled.

'I'm pretty sure I'd manage to get it in the back of the car,' he said again. 'Perhaps I could come in in the morning. Or are you open then?'

'I could be. What time would suit?'

'Half ten?'

It was agreed, and they left the confined space. As they did so, Imogen was hailed from afar by a large man and his wife who had just arrived. She excused herself and went to them. Jarvis watched her go.

'Glamorous widow,' said a voice beside him.

Jarvis turned. The voice, like the man, was small and nondescript, limply holding an almost empty glass. Jarvis hesitated, then remembered. 'Mr . . . Mr Nimbus, isn't it?' he asked.

'Verrry good,' said the small man. 'Yes. I am the black cloud.'

'With occasional bolts of lightning?' said Jarvis wryly.

Nimbus crinkled his eyes in acknowledgement. 'I can't remember your name, but I think you were here at the last opening weren't you?'

'Yes. I was.'

'And you're here again, Mr . . . ?'

'Jarvis.'

'So it was the woman that brought you last time?'

'No. Mr Turpin was my friend, but when the widow found I was to be in town again just now she invited me to the re-opening.'

'I see,' said the small man slowly. He finished his drink and looked hopefully around.

Cohen went past and smiled broadly at Jarvis.

'So you know him as well.' Nimbus paused. 'You wouldn't be here professionally, would you?'

'I beg your pardon?'

'I hear there's someone official up from London. Helping the police in investigating the death. That wouldn't be you, would it?'

'Would I tell you if it were?' laughed Jarvis.

'Of course you wouldn't,' came the reply. The small man smiled, took a couple of paces forward to intercept a waitress, and retreated holding a full glass of whisky. 'But if you were,' he went on as if without a break, 'someone like me might have something to say.'

'Go on.'

Nimbus smiled and sipped. 'Where did the money come from for this enterprise?' He flicked his eyes about the room.

'You told me that Ben's wife and her sister were well off.'

'They are. But where did it come from?'

'Their family, I believe.'

'Consider that question further,' said Nimbus, and took a large swallow from his glass.

'I don't know what you mean.'

'If you are what I think you are, you will be able to work things out a bit more. He'll help.' Nimbus pointed to where Cohen was talking to a couple.

'I don't know what you mean.'

'Sometimes a death can solve a cash-flow problem,' Nimbus said darkly, and made to move off towards the group with Cohen in it.

Jarvis caught his sleeve. 'You'll need to be more specific than that,' he said.

Nimbus focused beyond Jarvis, gave his head a slight shake. 'Shh!' he said softly, and then: 'Well, that's a very interesting point of view,' he added in normal conversational tones.

Jarvis found his own elbow taken.

'Excuse me,' Imogen Turpin said to Nimbus. 'There's someone I want you to meet,' she said to Jarvis, and towed him off. Then, as they walked together she added, 'I'm sorry. He's such a revolting little man, but Ben and he seemed to get on well, and I felt I just had to invite him. Now, come and meet the Careys.'

Making his way back to his car, Jarvis saw Cohen waiting for him.

'Something wrong?' he asked.

'I just wondered if you'd any thoughts after all that,' came the reply.

'Have you?'

'Yes.'

'Can I give you a lift?'

'Thanks. My car's just round the corner, but it would be better to be out of sight.'

'Of whom?'

Cohen jerked his head in the direction that Jarvis had come from. Jarvis unlocked his car and they got in.

'Well?' asked Jarvis. 'Where were you today?'

'Buena Vista was burgled, probably yesterday afternoon.' Jarvis was astonished and showed it.

'Happens all the time,' said Cohen. 'There's a death, and shortly after someone goes in thinking there'll be no one there, or that there'll be things lying around.'

'Anything taken?'

'Mrs T. says not. Oh, there's a considerable mess. Drawers thrown about and suchlike. Like they were looking for cash. But the TV and recorder were left, and they hadn't the sense to take the miniatures on the bedroom wall upstairs. I reckon it wasn't a professional job. Not a properly professional.' He sighed.

'She didn't seem too put out about it.' Jarvis jerked his head back in the direction of the Gallery.

'Nothing taken. Oh, she was shocked. But she's the kind that bounces back quickly. Re-opening the Gallery this soon shows that.' Cohen interlocked his fingers and flexed them.

Jarvis got the message. 'But that's not what you stopped to say?'

'No. I reckon that that's peripheral—unrelated. But I was talking to Nimbus before you were. He suggested that we should look into the financing of the Gallery.'

'That's what he said to me too.'

'He's got you tagged, hasn't he!' Cohen grinned.

'He seems quite good at putting things together.' Jarvis smiled and added hastily, 'Not that I conceded what he said.'

'Aye. That'll be right. Still, what d'you think?'

'It might be worth a look.'

'Good. I'm glad you agree. Come in tomorrow and I'll show you something.'

'OK. Later on. I've agreed to call at the Gallery and take that picture with me. Suppose you tell me what it's about?'

'It can wait. It can wait one night.'

'I suppose so. But a hint just now would let me think a bit first.'

'Well . . .' Cohen seemed reluctant. Then: 'Try this out. Was your friend Ben sufficiently well off when you knew him to burst into the art scene with a gallery of his own?'

There was a silence.

'That all?'

'Mix in anything else you know.'

'Know? Or do you mean "think", "speculate", or what.'

'I've a hunch!' Cohen put his hand on the door-handle.

'As the Goon Show used to say, "It suits you."' Jarvis smiled again. 'No offence. I know what you mean. I've got in trouble through not paying attention to hunches.'

'So've I.' Cohen said the words solemnly, opened the car door, and got out. He turned and put his head back in the door. 'There's something I forgot. Customs finally replied—after I'd phoned again. They've got no interest in your friend. Nor ever had. They want to know why we asked. Seem to think we know something they don't. I said I'd get back to them. What should we say?'

Jarvis thought briefly. 'Tell them it was just a random thought you considered worth following. Nothing serious.'

'Sure? They can be like rottweilers if they think there's something being kept back from them. Never let go.'

'It'll do for the present.'

Cohen looked at Jarvis—there had been a bleaknesss in his tone.

Jarvis started the engine without looking at him.

Back at his accommodation, Jarvis found himself chilling. He made himself a stiff brandy with sugar and hot water and sat for a few minutes watching the start of the late film. But then his nose began to run. He went to the bathroom and, without thinking, took one of the evening cold treatment pills he usually carried with him for such eventualities. It was not until he had swallowed that he remembered the brandy—and then, short of making himself sick, it was too late. But he reckoned that he'd not actually killed himself and went off to bed, where he fell deeply asleep.

CHAPTER 10

Wednesday

He woke early next morning with a mouth full of fur, his head muzzy. He decided another few minutes would make no difference. He next woke with a start, instinct making him immediately check his watch. He had twenty minutes to get to the Turpin Gallery.

Notwithstanding, breakfastless but shaven and punctual, at half past ten Jarvis arrived at the Gallery. He shook his coat to rid it of the light rain. Imogen Turpin appeared from behind the waist in the room, saw him and called. 'Oh, it's you. I've just got it wrapped up.' She went back out of sight.

Jarvis found her on her knees, putting string round the picture which was now wrapped in large sheets of brown paper.

'Finger?' she said, taking up the string.

'I really feel guilty about this.' He was apologetic. 'I do think you should keep it.'

'Nonsense,' she replied, putting the string round the parcel. 'We settled that last night. Finger?' And, when he had bent and complied with the request, she tied an expert knot. 'There!' She settled. 'That'll hold it. I thought it would be best wrapped in this weather.'

'Do you need a receipt?' he asked, getting to his feet.

'I don't think so,' she said. 'You are honest, aren't you?' She smiled roguishly up at him and held up her hand. He pulled her to her feet.

'I'll let you have a letter about it,' he said. 'Doubtless the lawyer will want something to put in his files.'

'All right. If you think that's necessary.' She looked carefully at him. 'Are you feeling all right?' she asked, and then with a smile: 'You look as though you enjoyed last night very well.'

'Yes, I did,' he replied. 'But this—' he pointed to his face—'is the onset of a cold, I think.'

'Oh, that's too bad. I do hope not. Summer colds are such a pest. Have you got anything for it?'

'I took something last night. On top of your wine it may not have been a good idea.' He bent and lifted the picture to the vertical, preparatory to picking it up.

'Are you to be staying in Glasgow long?' she asked, putting a hand on his arm.

'I'm not sure how much longer.'

'Are you still on business?' She was incredulous. 'There's not still some doubt about . . . about . . .' She turned away.

'I may have to come back down specially some other time,' he said. 'There's some loose ends that need tying up—administrative things.' He tried to reassure her.

'Ah well.' She turned back to face him and put both hands on his arm as he held the picture. 'Maybe, if you've some free time you'd like to come out with Tessa and me on the loch?' She smiled.

'Mm. That'd be good,' he said. 'It'd depend on the weather, I suppose.'

'Tessa and I go out quite a bit over summer irrespective of the weather. Give me a phone when you're free and I'll tell you which days are most likely.'

'Fine.' Then he remembered. 'I hear you'd a break-in.'

Her face clouded. 'Yes.'

'I am sorry. Much taken?'

She shook her head. 'No. It's just such an intrusion. There was such a mess. But I can't see anything of value's gone.'

'Maybe they were disturbed.'

'Yes. That may be it.' She sounded flat. 'I'll take an end.' She took the top of the picture.

He bent and hoisted the other end. Turpin's masterpiece was an awkward carry and they had trouble fitting it into the capacious Volvo station-wagon. For safety he had to let down the rear seat to get it in.

Back at his pied-à-terre he unwrapped the *Icarus*, propped it up against an easy chair, put the fire on and went to the kitchen.

Returning, he sat with a mug of tea and gazed at the picture. After a few moments he went on his knees beside it for a closer look. Yes: his eyes were not playing tricks. There were two tiny figures, one smaller than the other, on a rock overlooking the sea that Icarus was falling into. The larger figure was skirted.

He went back to his chair. He had no recollection of figures other than Icarus and Daedalus when he had seen the picture before. But then, on neither occasion had he really scrutinized it. Those times had been matters of impression: now he looked with proprietary eyes.

After another few minutes he put the *Icarus* out of sight behind the sofa and fetched the paintings Lynn had given him. These he also propped against a chair, although getting the unframed picture to stand proved a little awkward. He hitched himself closer to inspect the smaller watercolours. It wasn't enough. He brought them closer and sat with them close to his feet. He smiled, remembering Cohen's comment about the acquisitive effect of looking down at paintings.

Finally he pulled the sofa round from the wall, put it close to his chair and arranged the pictures against it, *Goat Fell* on his left, *Icarus* in the middle and *Ben Lomond* to the right. He fetched another mug of tea, and sat opposite them, cradling it in his hands, his elbows on his knees looking from one to the other before settling back into his chair.

An hour later he woke. His mug had fallen from his hands and stained the carpet. He muttered an oath, and fetched a cloth.

2

'You all right?' Cohen asked when Jarvis showed up in mid-afternoon. 'You look as bad as I feel.'

'I think so. I was a bit shivery overnight, but it'll maybe pass.'

'I hope you've not brought the 'flu.' Cohen looked keenly at the other.

'No. It's just a cold. And I was unaware enough to put a cold medicine on top of last night's hospitality.'

'Well, I hope it's not the 'flu. There's a lot of it about in the schools. I hope you're not in here infecting us all.' Cohen was clearly not convinced.

'You'll get pills for it, if necessary.' Jarvis smiled. 'You said last night you'd got something for me to read?'

Cohen nodded, and went to his filing cabinets. 'You can use that table,' he said, 'unless you want to go up to the Conference Room. I don't think it's in use. Have you had any thoughts overnight?' He gave Jarvis no chance to reply to the question, however. Swinging round with a file in his hand, 'Better read this first,' he said.

'Is that all?' asked Jarvis, making a pretence of weighing the file.

Half an hour later Jarvis closed the file, put his hands behind his head and stared up at the ceiling. The Conference Room was well-appointed, high ceilinged yet somehow impersonal, alien. There was too much glass and steel.

He felt a familiar shiver, not the cold, but a sudden feeling of dawning recognition. Now, he thought. Now! Things were moving. There was something here. No pattern yet, but he felt the familiar tingle. Then he stopped. Shiver? Maybe a hot drink would be useful. He headed for the canteen.

'You look a lot better,' grunted Cohen as Jarvis came back into his room. 'Just a minute.' He went out with a sheet of paper in his hand. Jarvis waited.

'Well?' asked Cohen as he came back into the room and shut the door.

'Something wrong?' Jarvis thought Cohen looked upset.

The other man took a deep breath, and then let it out. 'No. It's nothing—nothing concerning you. Just some office incompetence.' He sat down. 'Well? What do you make of that?' He pointed to the file that Jarvis still held.

'Why didn't you show me this earlier?' Jarvis put the file down on Cohen's desk.

'One answer might be: I still don't know whether you're here to help or hinder.' Cohen saw Jarvis purse his lips and, leaning forward, continued quickly. 'The real answer is that I hadn't thought of it till yesterday afternoon. It was only a chance comment by someone round the office that got me to get the file out of store.'

'Who?'

'One of the lads that had been on that investigation.' He pointed a finger at the file.

'Mm?'

'We'd been talking in the canteen. Usual stuff. "Things go in threes." You know the sort of thing. He wondered who'd be the third death connected with the Wintergreens of Balgarnock.'

'Balgarnock's the old railway works?'

'That's right. Charlie's a steam railway buff, and these folk all seem to know what the heirs of the famous families are still doing. He made the connection between the two deaths. Entirely innocently. "Who'll be the third death?" he said. But when I got the file out . . .' Cohen shrugged.

'What do you make of it?'

'So—correct me if I'm wrong—David Bruce was the husband of one of the Wintergreen twins, Tessa. And Ben married the other, Imogen.'

'Right.'

'I seem to remember Nimbus saying the Wintergreen daughters were from a family that had been wealthy, but the father had dissipated the cash that was left in the coffers.'

Cohen nodded. 'The Wintergreens' financial reputation was not well-based, shall we say? Though they still managed to move in the richer circles of Glasgow.'

'And Bruce was an entrepreneur—whatever that means.'

Cohen nodded. 'It means he made a lot of money rather quickly.'

'Why did he marry someone whom he must have known was not well off?'

'You've seen the sisters. There are some things only glands explain!'

Jarvis conceded the point with a smile. 'Bruce was heavily insured. He went boating with his wife and his sister-in-law and her husband, Ben. Bruce fell overboard and in the excitement of an attempted rescue, he was hit by an oar and fractured his skull. That, rather than drowning, was the cause of death.'

'Correct.'

Jarvis started to laugh, and, seeing Cohen's expression, explained. 'Over a year ago, at the Gallery's first opening, Nimbus said to me that such a thing as an oar had not entered Bruce's head before. I get the reference now—it's that old poem about David and Goliath. "Sic a thing as a chuckle stane had ne'er entered Goliath's heid."' Cohen's expression changed little. 'Forget it.' Jarvis gave up explaining.

'I'm glad you're amused,' stated Cohen.

'But maybe that's where the money came from for the Gallery—that's what Nimbus was hinting at last night.' Jarvis gazed into space. Cohen sat silent, waiting.

'And you're not dismissing the possibility.'

Cohen waited.

'And you're thinking that there are parallels with Ben's death.'

Cohen spread his hands, grimaced and shrugged.

'Except—' Jarvis got to his feet and went to the window, looked out briefly, then turned back to Cohen—'except that Ben wasn't insured. So far as anyone knew.'

'We've only got Imogen Turpin's word for that.'

Jarvis sat, draped his arm over the back of the chair and bit at his thumb pensively. 'I suppose that's true. Maybe she thought he had insured after she had urged him to get himself covered. Certainly, when I spoke to her, she was very definite that he wasn't insured; but I suppose if she thought him insured, and then he proved not to be, that would be a big disappointment.'

'He might have told her he'd got himself insured just for the sake of peace.'

'True.'

'In which case she'd have been really upset to find out he wasn't.'

'She wasn't that upset,' said Jarvis slowly. 'Not as upset as I would expect someone would be in those circumstances.' Then he added at a normal pace: 'But I suppose I saw her a while after she'd have found there was no insurance. She'd have got over the shock of the news by then. Or at least would be able to conceal it.'

Cohen snorted gently and waved a finger. 'Or maybe it's just your charm. I saw her cosying up to you on Tuesday.'

'She's invited me out boating,' said Jarvis quietly. 'In any case—' he shifted in his seat—'aren't we making some large and unjustified assumptions?'

'That's true.' Cohen settled back in his seat.

Jarvis leaned forward. 'So, if what you're thinking is right, we've got two murders and not one.'

Cohen shrugged.

'And we've got the same motive for each?'

'Money,' said Cohen, with relish.

'There could be other motives,' Jarvis said slowly.

'Such as?'

'Sex. What if La Imogen wanted to go off with, say, one of those young men who were hovering last night. Or, more plausibly, what about jealousy? What if Ben were on the verge of going off with someone?' He paused, remembering the woman in the house next door to Buena Vista.

'What if Turpin was about to confess to the earlier murder?' Cohen cut across Jarvis's thought.

'You're very sure of that—it is only a remote hypothesis.'

'But you didn't laugh at it.'

'No, I didn't.'

'Why not?' Cohen was urgent.

'I read the statements. All three survivors said they couldn't swim. That was why they were trying to push an oar at the deceased. The oar that hit him. Poleaxed him, more like.'

'And?'

Jarvis sat back, shook his head and sighed. 'Ben could

swim like a fish. When we were students he and I got our gold for life-saving at the same time. He reminded me of that when the Gallery was first opened—last year.'

Cohen and he looked at each other.

'Well,' said Cohen. 'That's something.'

Jarvis went back to the flat. Having eaten, he dug out his sheets of A4 and started re-jigging his thoughts. He put another couple of question-marks beside the word 'Drugs', and then took another sheet. What was the possibility of there having been two murders—Ben's and his brother-in-law's?

He tried to list the similarity: Widow. Sisters. ?Insurance. He looked at this last and added another question-mark—?Insurance?

It wasn't getting very far.

He drew a line and started again with a fresh sheet of A4. IMOGEN, he printed. Then underneath he wrote 'Motive': What were the standard motives? Money and sex. Were there any other? He brainstormed, writing down anything that seemed possible. He could go over the ideas and sift them later.

Shortly he had listed under 'Motive': money, freedom, threat from Ben, jealousy, other men. Then he drew an arrow, taking 'threat from Ben' to the bottom of the list.

Money—he drew a line out from the word and wrote '?insurance'. Then: 'Did she know or not?'

Freedom—what had he meant by that? Just that Imogen might have wanted to be free, not to marry or live with someone else, but just to be free. After all, it seemed her sister had not remarried. Perhaps that was an example of a freedom that Imogen had wanted also.

Jealousy—well, Ben always had had a roving eye. Presumably he hadn't grown out of it. There might be something there. Wide eyes floated into Jarvis's memory as he wrote down 'Neighbour'.

Other men—he tapped his pen on the paper. That he did not know. But again his mind supplied a name. Maurice. He drew another line from the name—?pictures?

Threat from Ben—disclosure of Bruce death? But that wouldn't have helped Ben. Unless the financing of the new Gallery had come from the Bruce sister and maybe Ben was asking for more. But how would Ben have been able to put pressure on her? He drew another line and a circle which he left empty.

Then he drew a line under the listing and looked at the paper again.

Two ideas seemed more possible than the others and worth following first. He wrote and circled two words: 'Neighbour' and 'Paris'.

CHAPTER 11

Thursday

'You want me to go to France? Just like that?' Cohen was flabbergasted.

'That's right,' said Jarvis. 'You've got a passport, haven't you?'

'Of course I've got a passport. But I can't just go off like that!'

'I'm sure if you tell your bosses it's at my request, there'll be no problem. Or do you want me to ask for you?'

'No. That will not be necessary.' Cohen was mildly indignant. Clearly he would fight his own battles.

'You said you'd a contact over there dealing with pictures.'

'Yes.'

'Well, phone him and make an appointment.' Jarvis paced about. 'Make it for the late morning. Half twelve or so. It'll take us a while to get into Paris from Charles de Gaulle. I've organized currency and got us somewhere to stay. Unless you've got some favourite place of your own.' He smiled quizzically.

'Well . . .'

'Give me a note and we'll see what we can do,' said Jarvis.

'No, I've got nowhere special. I didn't mean that. It's just I don't see why me. Why don't you go on your own?'

'You're the art expert. That's part of it. But there's another point,' replied Jarvis. 'You've got an official link into the police that I don't have, and I don't want to activate an alternative route to their cooperation unless it is really necessary. It isn't necessary if you go with me. In any event, the possibility of a French connection with those pictures you mentioned is something that has to be excluded.'

'You do just mean pictures, do you?' asked Cohen. 'There's the other meaning of "French connection".'

'I do just mean pictures,' Jarvis assured him. Then he checked himself. He had forgotten something. 'Will it be all right with your wife?' he asked. 'I should have thought of that before.'

Cohen shrugged.

'Is she working? Do you want to take her? We'll have to stay the night. I don't think we can do it in one day. The plane back's at six, which'd mean we'd have to leave for De Gaulle about four-thirty to be safe. There's no way we could be sure of being free by then. So probably there'd be some free time the next day for sightseeing. And there's the evening.'

'She's a teacher. No, it doesn't matter. I've had to go off before on other police matters, sometimes at shorter notice than this.'

'I'm sorry,' said Jarvis. 'But in any case, come to think about it, you'd need to pay her fare yourself. I can't do anything about that.'

Cohen nodded. 'I know. I've paid for her a couple of times.' He relaxed. 'We've had a couple of holidays there—long weekends. They're quite cheap through one of the travel agents—Sheila found out about them.'

'That's when you saw that Picasso Museum you were telling me about?'

'Yes.'

'Will she let you go on your own? Let you loose in Paris?' Jarvis's tone was jocular.

'She'll be all right. It's only for a couple of days. Besides, there's the kids to be looked after. We couldn't drop them on the grandparents at that short notice, and in any case the school's too far away from where they are.'

'OK. That's good,' said Jarvis. 'I'm glad that'll work.'

'Well,' said Cohen, picking up his phone, 'I'll make arrangements.'

'I've done that travel-wise. We've to go Business Class—there was no room Economy. You just need to fix up your contact.'

Cohen replaced his receiver. 'Any other shocks you've got for me?' he asked. 'I prefer to have only one a day.'

'Actually, yes. There is something. Would the Turpin Gallery be open now?' asked Jarvis.

'The Gallery? Why d'you want to go haring round there? I could find out.'

'No,' said Jarvis. 'It's not the Gallery. I just would like to know where Imogen Turpin is when we make a visit to her next-door neighbour.'

'Her neighbour?'

Jarvis explained.

2

As he drove to Drymen, Cohen said in conversational tones, 'I came up with another hypothesis last night. Maybe you've got it in your list?'

'Oh yes? What's that?'

'The first wife.'

'Oh?' As Cohen spoke Jarvis realized he had not considered Lynn when he had been making out that listing. Why not? He had tried to brainstorm—to list everything even remotely possible: yet his mind had failed to come up with her name, despite the Rowardennan picture. He had a sinking feeling that maybe he had tried to spare himself sorrow.

Cohen caught the guarded note in Jarvis's voice, and

glanced at him briefly before a corner took his attention. It was some seconds before he spoke again. 'I just wondered if she thought that there was a fat insurance on Turpin, and thought some of it might come her way—somehow or other.' He risked another glance.

Silence.

'You said you were sweet on her one time.'

More silence.

'My old instructor used to say you've got to look at all angles.' There was no apology in Cohen's tones.

'Mm. Sure. But let's get this out of the way first.' Jarvis pointed ahead.

The garage at Buena Vista was open and empty as they drew up beside its neighbour. This was also open and was better fitted out, with garden equipment hanging neatly, tool-racks and a Work-mate bench. Cohen got out of the car and walked across to the fence between the two gardens.

'Interesting,' he said, twanging the wire.

A woman came out of the back door behind them. She was dressed in blue slacks with a matching top.

'What do you think you're doing?' she asked frostily.

Jarvis recognized her as he got out of the car. She had been in the garden before when he had been out to Buena Vista. His impression of her attractiveness was confirmed. He and Cohen went over to her.

'We're police officers, ma'am,' said Cohen, producing his card and showing it to her. 'I wonder if we might have a word in private.'

'What about?' Her eyes flashed.

'We're investigating the death of Mr Turpin,' Cohen replied.

'Oh.' Suddenly she was confused. 'You'd better come in.' She led the way through the kitchen to the lounge at the front of the house. To Jarvis's eyes it was the mirror image of the one in Buena Vista. There were bowls of flowers on low tables. Fuchsias and geraniums were patches of colour in a long low frame immediately in front of the window. Model ships and railway engines stood in plastic boxes on top of the bookcase and on a shelf in the display cabinet which was otherwise filled with china.

The woman sat down in a white leather arm chair and motioned Jarvis and Cohen to seats. She first slumped and then quickly sat up, still and watchful, her hands on each arm of the chair, red nails stark against the white. She's like a Siamese cat, Jarvis found himself thinking. Indeed, he would have bet that she was Eurasian somewhere in her background.

She looked at Cohen, then at Jarvis and nodded quietly. 'You were here before,' she said to him.

'Next door,' said Jarvis.

'That's right. I remember.'

'Mrs . . . ?' began Cohen.

'Andrews.'

Jarvis was seated beside a glass-topped wooden-framed low square table. On it were a silver ashtray and a large photograph in a white-leather mount. A man in some sort of uniform smiled from it, while behind him rose the Rock of Gibraltar.

'Mrs Andrews,' said Cohen firmly, 'we're trying to build up some picture of Mr Turpin's background—what he was like, and so on. We were wondering if you could cast any light—living next door there might be something you would know that we wouldn't otherwise come across . . .' Cohen's voice trailed off again. Jarvis checked the grin that threatened to erupt on his face. Cohen's salesman father would have been proud of his son.

'I'm not sure if there's anything I know that's worth mentioning,' replied Mrs Andrews.

'Can I ask how long you've been living here?' Cohen continued.

'Three years. We—my husband and I—moved in just as the Turpins did. The houses were new.'

'I see. And did you get to know the Turpins at all?'

'Not really.'

'Not—not at all?'

She nodded, looking first at Cohen and then at Jarvis, who sat impassive.

'Which?'

'I knew them to see them, of course. But that was about the extent of it.'

'Did you get to know Mrs Turpin? Two housewives up here out of the way together, you must have got to know Mrs Turpin?'

'No.' The answer was flat and brief. Her lips thinned.

'And Mr Turpin?'

'Not really. He used to wave as he went out, but she put a stop to that.'

'I see.' Cohen looked at Jarvis, clearly passing the questioning over to him.

Jarvis smiled and gestured at the photographs beside him. 'Your husband?'

'Yes.'

'Gibraltar?'

'Yes.' She smiled.

'He does the models, does he?'

She nodded. 'He's got quite a good workshop out in the garage. And he brings them home too. It's his hobby.'

'Did you meet out there?'

'Yes.' Mrs Andrews was clearly surprised that Jarvis was persisting on that line.

'Is he Air Force?'

She smiled a small smile of contempt. 'He was.'

'And now?'

'He's gone east for a while. It pays well just now.'

'Forgive me asking, but you did say you met out there?' Jarvis indicated the Gibraltar backdrop. 'It's an interesting place.'

'Yes. Actually we did. Tom was on duty, and I was out with the Army Corps.' She laughed lightly at their expressions, for she did not seem to them like a serving Army person. 'Daddy was Army, so I followed suit.'

'But not now.'

'Oh no. Not now.'

'How do you pass the time?'

She smiled at Jarvis, who leaned forward in his chair.

121

Then she turned her head and gestured at the plants in the window display.

'Are you much of a gardener?' asked Jarvis quietly.

Mrs Andrews's head came round quickly. 'I enjoy my garden.'

'It looks very well. Do you have much trouble with water over summer, or is there a good water table?'

She relaxed a bit. 'It's pretty well watered, really. It seems to come down the slope. I've never had to water in the three years we've been here.'

'Do you do it all yourself?' He looked down at her hands.

She laughed. 'We got it laid out professionally when we came in, and I manage.'

'And you wear gloves.'

She nodded, waggling her red square finger-nails. To Jarvis's eyes she had good gardener's hands. 'Of course.'

'Any plants you specially like?' He turned to look at the pot plants. 'I used to grow fuchsias, but never as well as these.'

'Those certainly. I've got a greenhouse at the back of the garden.' She was proud.

Jarvis sighed. 'I used to work with Ben Turpin. Before. Indeed, it goes back further than that. We were at University together. We were good friends.' He turned back to the woman. 'I understand that Ben used to spend time out in his garage with his hang-glider. I find it hard to believe that he wouldn't have said "hello" over the fence.' He spoke with a certain calm world-weariness, staring at her. 'Has your husband been away long?'

She stared back. Her hands still on the white leather, clenched slowly as the implied question sank in.

'Well,' said Cohen as they drove back to Glasgow. 'That's as neat a job as I've ever seen blown. And I've seen plenty, I can tell you.'

Jarvis shook his head almost angrily. 'I'm sorry,' he said. Then he took a deep breath and added, 'I got it wrong. She's still behind?'

Cohen glanced into the rear-view mirror. 'Yes.' He gave

his attention to his driving for a few hundred yards and then spoke emphatically. 'Maybe you didn't get it wrong, but you've certainly messed it up for the present. I just hope she doesn't complain officially.'

'All right! All right! I said I'm sorry. But why are you getting a statement from her? Surely we should just have backed away with apologies.'

Cohen snorted. 'Look. I'm protecting us in case she does complain. There's bound to be something in the statement to justify our speaking to her. That'll get us off the hook if she makes a fuss.'

'Why her car?' Jarvis jerked his head to indicate the following vehicle.

'D'ye think I want you and her in the same vehicle?'

There was silence for a period. Jarvis mused, then said slowly, 'A statement could have other uses.'

'How do you mean?'

'We're still left with a motive why Imogen Turpin might want to see her husband dead.' Jarvis was bleak, looking out of the passenger window as they started to come down through rows of neat, small bungalows. 'If she suspected something—was jealous. You know. Even if there was nothing going on, as Andrews says.'

'It might also leave us with a reason why Andrews would have been the one to sabotage the glider. Perhaps it's she that's lying. Perhaps he didn't make a play for her, like you thought. Maybe he turned her down.'

'Logically possible, but unlikely,' replied Jarvis. 'Not if I know Ben. Not if he'd the chance. In any case, if that were so she'd not say so. Not to us, at any rate. But there's another point. Did you see her hands? I'm not sure those hands could have tackled a wire job.'

'She's got an Army training. I wonder if those nails are glued on.' Cohen braked suddenly as a dog came across the carriageway.

'I doubt it.'

Cohen pursed his lips. 'Long-sighted, are you?'

Jarvis ignored the comment. 'In any event it just doesn't fit. Not now. Oh, I suppose if the glider were stored in the garage with its door open as Imogen Turpin said, Andrews could have come over the fence and tampered with it. But maybe not. Imogen, now—she's much more likely.'

'Or maybe that repair was done by Turpin himself.'

'Certainly that's what Imogen indicated. She said he had been tinkering with it.'

'Blast!' said Cohen suddenly.

'Blast what?'

'I meant to check. It seemed to me that the wire from that fence looked newish. I wonder if it's what was on the glider. Oh well, I'll get someone to go out and have a look. Or we could go back out this afternoon.'

'I'd prefer not to be involved.'

'Why?'

Jarvis made a fluttering motion with his hand. 'It's not the right time to get too visible. We may want to surprise her. I wouldn't want her forewarned or forearmed in any way. That way you'd get the full benefit of the natural reaction.'

'Just like back there?' Cohen smiled bleakly.

Jarvis leaned forward to look in the passenger wing-mirror. 'She's still there?'

'Yes.'

'Well, let's hope her statement is adequate. It just may fit a pattern.'

'Pattern?'

'Jig-saw. My great-aunt used to say once you get the feel of the pattern a jigsaw goes much quicker. It was her hobby,' he added unnecessarily.

3

Once Mrs Andrews's statement had been typed up and signed she left. Cohen looked at it bleakly and passed it to Jarvis. 'Well,' he said. 'Scratch Mrs Emma Andrews. Like I said, I just hope she doesn't complain. She looks like a strong woman.' He pointed at the signature which was in a flowing bright blue. 'The graphologists say those kind of folk are bad to cross.'

Jarvis nodded, and handed the sheet back.

They headed for the canteen. Jarvis grimaced as he looked at the menu, and eventually settled for mince and a little mealie with chips. 'I'll probably pay for this,' he grumbled to Cohen, 'but there's nothing else worth eating.'

'Gut trouble?'

'Occasionally. I had an ulcer some years back, and usually I watch it. It's all right most of the time, but work like this gets me going, and chips and mealie will probably put me back on the antacids by mid-afternoon.' He patted his jacket as he spoke, checking that he had antacids with him.

'I can eat anything,' said Cohen flatly, gesturing to the serving lady to put some roast potatoes as well as chips on his plate.

'Lucky you,' grinned Jarvis. 'I hope you stay that way.'

'Still,' said Cohen picking up his tray and following Jarvis to a table. 'I don't really see where the stress comes in. You just work things out and that's that.'

'You've never made a mistake?'

Cohen shrugged. 'Sometimes you get things wrong for a bit, but I've never had a case that I wasn't satisfied with—whether or not the result was a conviction.'

'You weren't in the Force when capital punishment was possible?'

'No. But I see what you're going to ask next. No. I don't think that'd make any difference to me either. It'd be up to the prosecution—Crown Office—to decide whether what we put to them grounded a capital charge.'

Jarvis nodded. That was the answer he'd expect from Cohen. Do your job to the limit that you were required to, and then hand on responsibility if that was the next step. 'I've made two mistakes,' said Jarvis bleakly.

Cohen looked at him, but Jarvis was clearly not going to say more, and his mind was somewhere else.

They ate their meal in silence.

CHAPTER 12

Friday–Saturday

Paris was overcast, hot and sticky. Jarvis had forgotten the difference six hundred miles can make.

Cohen shook his head as he sat down beside him, and pulled at his heavy tweed jacket. 'You might have warned me,' he complained.

'The water'll help,' said Jarvis. He himself was feeling fine; the heat seemed to have coped with his threatened 'flu.

They had dropped their overnight bags at the modest hotel that had been arranged for them, and were on their way to an appointment at the main Préfecture de Police on the Ile de la Cité. After a brief glance at his pocket map to refresh his memory, Jarvis had suggested they take a water-bus along the Seine from near the Eiffel Tower. They were waiting for one to arrive and making use of a drinks stall down on the embankment beside the jetty. Cohen had taken off his jacket and dropped gratefully into one of the white plastic seats in the shade of an umbrella. The heat beat out of the white stonework.

'It's an odd city,' said Jarvis ruminatively, gesturing with a can of citron at the tall blocks of flats across the river.

'Pity we're only here for the one night,' remarked Cohen.

'I thought you weren't keen to be too long away from home.'

'Once you're here you see things a bit different.'

'That's what I'm hoping,' said Jarvis quietly.

Away to their left a train went across the elevated track above the Bir Hakim bridge.

'Looks awful, doesn't it,' said Cohen, motioning towards where a large plastic bottle and other rubbish floated past on the muddy brown water.

'Sometimes I think plastic's the greatest curse of this

century,' said Jarvis. 'Maybe that's why it's a term of abuse. "Plastic"!'

'What are you hoping to find out?' asked Cohen, mopping his brow.

'I'm not sure,' replied Jarvis. His tone forbade further questions. He was now wrestling with a knotty problem: when should he tell Cohen about the insurance policy on Ben's life? The question had lain in his mind all through the flight, but there had not been opportunity to talk business. Now they could. What should he say? 'By the way, I've discovered I'm getting thirty thousand pounds because Ben's dead?' That would hardly do. Should he withdraw from the investigation as he now had an interest? Probably. But then, if there was a mystery he owed it to Ben to do what he could.

Cohen sensed something was bothering him and looked at Jarvis closely. He was about to speak when some chattering children occupied the next table. He sank back in the sun.

A river-boat came into view on the other side of the stream and turned towards the jetty. It rolled as it butted its way across the flow.

'Got your sea-sick pills?' asked Jarvis.

Cohen pursed his lips.

'At least it'll be cooler on the water,' Jarvis said, picking up his jacket.

Forty minutes later they were deep in conference in a small office in the police headquarters on the Ile de la Cité.

'It is true,' said the thin French detective as they concluded their conversation, 'that M. Maurice is someone we have on the occasion wondered about. But nothing more than that.'

'But you are not entirely surprised at the nature of our inquiries?' asked Jarvis.

Claude-Michel Amiel inclined his head and shrugged delicately. 'In this business one is never surprised, is one?'

'Yet you are surprised that he has a business contact as far away as Glasgow?' asked Cohen.

'Yes. I mean, no. After all was not your Glasgow the

successor of Paris as European City of Culture?' The French smile was sly. Cohen frowned.

'Well, I suppose the next thing to do is to go along and see if we can talk to him,' said Jarvis, rising to his feet.

'I am sorry I cannot be of more assistance,' said the Frenchman, as he came round his desk. 'But if we can assist, please ask.'

'Thanks, Claude,' said Cohen. 'We will.'

2

'I've not been as neatly stonewalled for a long time,' exploded Cohen once they were back out on the street.

Jarvis sighed. 'I didn't expect anything else. After all we're hardly a high priority in a place like this.' He waved a hand all around. 'But at least he didn't warn us off.'

'So.'

'So now we go and see M. Maurice.' He looked about him checking his bearings, then set off.

Half a mile later, Cohen had a question. 'What about lunch?' he asked.

'Good idea,' said Jarvis. 'There's no point getting there until Maurice is open, and I bet he lunches till about two-thirty if not three.'

They ate at a pavement café, sharing a spaghetti bolognaise despite the heat, and a carafe of white wine.

'I don't really see why we're here.' Cohen returned to his earlier question as they lingered over coffee. He had taken his jacket off again and rolled up his sleeves. He seemed to be enjoying himself.

'Are you objecting?'

'No. You call the shots. But . . . ?' His voice tailed off into the question.

'You remember I told you that Ben had had some problem with one of his French connections.'

'Yes.'

'Well, it seemed to me necessary to check out the French

end of the story. Elementary fairness.' Jarvis spread his hands with almost Gallic expressiveness.

Cohen looked carefully at him. 'It still doesn't seem worth spending heaven knows how much on taking the two of us over here. Someone local could have done it through Interpol.'

'Takes too long.'

'I didn't know that time is important.'

'Ah.' Jarvis did not explain. 'Well, when we see Maurice, perhaps I should do the talking.'

They fell silent.

After a few minutes Cohen began to fidget.

'Plenty of time,' said Jarvis.

'It's not that. I was just thinking it was odd that Turpin left you that picture.' He sat forward, willing to talk.

'A joke, I think.'

'Odd sense of humour.'

'He was like that.' Jarvis paused. Was this the time to mention that insurance policy? Perhaps not. It might take Cohen's mind off the ensuing interview, and that was not a good idea. Two independent minds would often provide what amounted to a binocular vision of an interview, highlighting things which a monocular view would not reveal. He sat silent, letting the pause die.

Cohen saw it die, and slouched back in his seat watching the passers-by.

After a while Cohen looked at his watch. 'Should we be going?'

Jarvis looked at his watch in turn and signalled the waiter. 'Yes. You're right. But I think I want to go back and get a print. It's been niggling away while we've been here, and I'm getting too old now to question my hunches.'

'As you please. Have we far to go?'

'No.'

3

They walked east along the Rue de Rivoli past the shoe and leather shops, to the small cafés and well-stocked food and wine shops in the less touristy part beyond the Hôtel de

Ville. Opposite St Paul's Church they headed left into the Marais. Jarvis took his map out of his pocket once more.

'Just a minute,' said Cohen suddenly. 'I think I know where we are.' He tugged a Berlitz from his pocket and checked. 'The Picasso Museum's somewhere over there.' He waved roughly in the direction they were headed.

'Well, it's not marked on my map,' remarked Jarvis.

'It only opened recently. Maybe you've got an old edition.'

'Maybe. Tell you what, if we've time after we've seen Maurice, we'll go and look at it.'

'Fine.'

'Meantime we go this way.' Jarvis pointed.

Maurice's gallery was not unlike Turpin's in décor and, though broader and not as long, had the same waisted design.

'That's where he got it,' breathed Jarvis as they entered the door.

'What? What've you seen?'

'Look at the layout and the colours.'

Cohen considered, nodded briefly, then shrugged. 'I see what you mean. But, fair's fair. Maybe it's over here that's copied from the Glasgow shop.' He broke off as a door opened in the back right-hand-side wall and a young woman came forward.

'Messieurs?' She smiled.

'Could we speak to M. Maurice?' Jarvis asked in indifferent French.

'I am afraid he is at lunch, but we expect him immediately,' she replied in faintly accented English. 'Do you wish to look until he comes? Or have you some specific picture in mind?'

'Thanks. We'll wait, if that's all right.' Jarvis retreated into English.

'As you wish.' She indicated that the gallery was at their disposal. 'Would you excuse me?' She disappeared back where she had come from.

Jarvis sighed. 'It takes me weeks to get into the way of French,' he lamented.

'Yours is better than mine, at least,' said Cohen as he drifted over to inspect the offerings on the walls.

The pictures were well framed and well hung. Many were late nineteenth-century and early twentieth-century rural landscapes, pleasant rather than startling. Fields and orchards, corn and poppies, were prevalent.

Cohen walked slowly past the exhibits, nodding as he went, while Jarvis stood near the door, looking at a broader, larger canvas that was on a special stand angled towards the window. Then he inspected two modern sculpture pieces made out of scrap metal and wire that stood in the corners of the window. They were about three feet high, and might have been a pair—he could not tell. One reminded him of Picasso's Don Quixote doodles. And if that was so, the other might have been Sancho Panza.

'Come and see this,' said Cohen suddenly. He had gone past the waist in the middle of the gallery and was looking at a wall that was concealed from the front of the establishment. Jarvis joined him.

Cohen was standing in front of a large picture placed alone on the small area of wall. It was another of the Icarus story. Unlike the one in Turpin's gallery, however, this was an antique.

'When would you place that?' asked Jarvis.

Cohen lifted a shoulder. 'Dunno. There's things like that from early on. I suppose, though, it's probably eighteen-twenties or so. Reminds me of Delacroix.'

'Why not later than that, or earlier?'

'Earlier was cruder, and they were too busy glorifying their Revolution. It was afterwards they moved into the sort of history and mythology subjects.'

'And after?'

'Well, after and you're into Courbet and Monet and those folk. Quite a different style, and the subject'd be quite wrong for them.'

Jarvis looked solemnly at Cohen. 'You do know your stuff,' he said.

'I'm reliable.' A twitch at the corner of Cohen's mouth reassured Jarvis, and he realized he was getting to like the man.

The street door opened and a man came in. He was well dressed, his dark hair sleeked down. A small moustache graced the lip above a weak chin. He walked to the back of the gallery, nodded to the two, and went through the door in the side wall. Jarvis recognized him. He had been the voluble Frenchman at the opening of the Turpin Gallery, and there was another bell chiming at the back of Jarvis's mind.

'Maurice?' whispered Cohen.

'Perhaps.' Jarvis wanted time to think. 'Let's look at the rest of the exhibits.' He led the way, but before they had done other than glance at the modern pictures, the man reappeared.

'Can I help you?' he inquired. 'You were asking for me personally.'

They identified themselves.

Maurice professed himself astonished and devastated to hear the bald news of Turpin's death, and Jarvis was inclined to believe him. As Maurice ushered them into his small office behind the curtain wall, he wondered, however, whether Cohen shared his view. Cohen seemed tight-lipped.

'But I do not know why you are here giving me this information,' said Maurice as they settled into chairs. 'Is there some . . . some mystery about the death, or Ben's affairs or something?'

'Unfortunately we are having to examine Mr Turpin's business dealings, and since we understand that he did quite a lot of business with you, we thought it was perhaps easiest to come and ask you directly rather than to rely upon more indirect methods,' said Jarvis smoothly.

The Frenchman pursed his lips once or twice, came to a decision and went to a filing cabinet in the corner. There he extracted a bulky file.

'I can only assume,' he said, 'that you have heard of

the problem that arose between M. Turpin and myself regarding the sale of *The Wheatfield*.'

'Not in any detail,' Jarvis replied. 'Can you . . . ?' He gestured.

Maurice opened the file, laying it flat on his desk. 'This is the Turpin file,' he said. 'It contains the detail of our transactions since . . . since . . .' He turned to the front of the file. 'Since seven years, when we first began our association.'

'So you traded and dealt regularly with Mr Turpin.'

'Yes. It was to the profit of both of us. He had a market for Post-Impressionists, particularly French—minor ones, you would understand. The really important Post-Impressionists?—their work is always in galleries and among the Grand Collections, and Ben was not dealing into that market. But he could and did sell many nice lesser Post-Impressionists, if I can call them so.'

Jarvis smiled, conspiratorially acknowledging the coy manner in which Maurice put the point. These 'lesser' painters were a good way below the standard of the leaders of the school. 'Did he tell you where he was selling them?'

'Not really. I assume there is an interest in these paintings in Scotland.'

'And beyond,' said Cohen drily.

M. Maurice glanced at him, then resumed. 'A year ago almost, I consigned to him one of a pair of pictures so that a particular client might consider their purchase.'

'*The Wheatfield?*' asked Jarvis.

Maurice nodded. 'To my astonishment, Ben sold the single picture to the client for a sum well below half what one might expect for the two together. On a wall they would have complimented each other.' He spread his hands.

'Compl-e-mented.' Jarvis's correction was automatic, and resented. The corners of Maurice's mouth turned down.

'But if the picture was clearly sent for consideration—on approval—surely he hadn't the right to sell.' Cohen's tone was definite.

'Precisely!'

'And you were upset? Naturally you would be.' Jarvis had registered his error and sought to retrieve it.

Maurice eyed him coldly, and then decided to accept the implicit apology. 'Of course.'

'So you came to Glasgow to see what could be done?' Jarvis continued quietly.

'Yes.' Maurice was relaxing.

'There must have been much money at stake.'

'Indeed.' Maurice spread a palm.

'How much?' interjected Cohen.

Maurice flashed him a glance. 'Enough.'

'I'm sure there must have been,' interposed Jarvis. 'You must understand that we are ignorant of such things and would welcome the guidance of an expert like yourself.'

A brief smile passed across Maurice's face. He opened the file again and took out an envelope with some Polaroid pictures in it. He selected two of these, pushed them across the desk to Jarvis. 'These are *The Wheatfield* and *The Meadow*.' Their titles were descriptive, though the second could equally have been called *Cows in Pasture*. Maurice sat back, as if at attention. 'It is my opinion that separately these pictures might have fetched some twenty thousand francs each.'

'And together?'

'As a pair, probably . . . perhaps . . .' He mused, looking up at the ceiling. 'Eighty or a hundred thousand francs.' He stared briefly into Cohen's eyes, and then turned to Jarvis.

'Yes. I see. There is quite a difference,' said Jarvis. 'Naturally you had to discuss the matter with Mr Turpin. What happened then?'

'When I arrived he professed not to know what I was speaking of. He said it had been a straight sale. This is nonsense.'

'And?'

'I do not understand?'

'What happened then? Were there any efforts to retrieve the picture?'

'Ah! Yes. Of course. We went to see the purchaser. He

was . . . Mr McLintock.' Maurice turned to the file and pulled out a small sheet of paper. 'Here you are.' He handed it to Jarvis, who looked at it and passed it to Cohen, who took a note of the name and address.

'But the purchaser was not willing to return the goods.'

'No.'

'You did not think of selling him the other picture?'

'That was impossible. Naturally, having one of the pair, he was not willing to pay the price which would have been the balance of the total.'

'Eh?' Cohen had not followed the syntax.

Jarvis turned to him. 'Together the two pictures were worth, say, one hundred thousand francs. Mr McLintock already had one half of the pair for something less than a quarter that price. He wasn't willing to buy the other for more than seventy-five thousand francs.' He looked at Maurice.

'Precisely,' agreed Maurice.

'Even though you might have taken your price down a little to make the sale?'

Maurice gestured speakingly.

'So you lost a good deal of money,' continued Jarvis.

'I lost a good deal. And a lot of money.' Maurice nodded.

'Then what happened?'

'I was incensed.'

'Did you come to blows?'

'Monsieur, that question is not innocent. To ask it, you must know that I hit Monsieur Ben. Hard. He had the stitches.'

'You must have been very angry.' Jarvis's voice was quiet.

'I have the hot temper.'

Both Jarvis and Cohen looked solemnly at Maurice. After a few seconds of their staring, he shifted in his seat, looking first at one and then the other. 'You are not thinking . . . ? How exactly did Ben die?'

Jarvis explained concisely. Turpin had had an accident while hang-gliding.

Maurice relaxed. 'I see. For the moment I thought there was some question as to whether his death had been . . .

assisted. And that you were thinking my dispute with him was . . . part of it.'

'There is some question whether the accident was all that it seemed,' Jarvis responded.

Maurice stiffened again. 'And you think that I . . . ?' He got to his feet. 'It is preposterous. Yes, we had the quarrel. But that happens between business associates, even those that know each other well.'

'I was going to ask when and how you became acquainted with M. Turpin,' said Jarvis.

'We were friends from years back. When he was working with the British Embassy, or was it the British Council, here in Paris. Years ago.'

'Before he was in the art business?'

'Oh yes. It was after he went into the art business as you call it—' the distaste for the phrase hung in the air—'that he got in touch. He was then in London, and we did some trading. When he went to Glasgow, our arrangement continued.'

'And the arrangement was . . . ? I don't mean detail, but how did the arrangement work?'

Maurice sat down again, and closed the file on the desk. He leaned over it, hands clasped together. 'You will understand that the question of market is very important in keeping prices for works of Art at a proper level.'

Jarvis nodded.

'Ben, my friend, was opening a new market. In London there were those who were interested in French art—at the right price, of course. It was the same in Glasgow. I understand that he was able to interest Americans. So many Americans, it seems, go to Scotland. They feel affection for that gloomy country.' Maurice shrugged his own opinion. 'And when they are there they buy pictures.'

'But surely they would be buying Scottish scenes,' Cohen interjected. 'If the purpose was to remind them of their roots.'

Maurice smiled. 'They want pictures that they like. So we supply them.'

'Post-Impressionists?' asked Jarvis.

'Indeed.'

'I would have thought there were not all that many Post-Impressionists going around now—that all that were painted were now in galleries or in collectors' hands.'

'There are always some available if one knows where to look.'

Cohen suddenly leaned forward, his forearm on Maurice's desk. 'You and he wouldn't have found a new supply?' he asked.

'We have never sold a picture with a false attribution.'

'What about "in the style of"? Would that count as an attribution?'

'But no. Of course not.' Maurice smiled. 'And we would not sell such pictures for the same price as the work of a Master.'

Cohen waved a hand to encompass the whole of Paris. 'It strikes me that in a city like this there might be quite a few people able to turn out pictures for you. I seem to remember some competent Post-Impressionist work being painted and for sale up beside Sacré-Cœur.' He turned back to Maurice and pointed a finger at him. 'So how many have you shipped through Turpin to poor ignorant Americans?'

Maurice spread his hands and smiled blandly. 'We have done nothing wrong. People want pleasant pictures which reflect their ideas—their feelings—about the countryside. Idealized perhaps, but genuine. We supply them. Pastoral scenes, with some touches of an older way of life. The orchard with the cart, the cattle going to the milking. It is harmless.'

Jarvis nodded. He had the picture. It was typical of Turpin.

'You, of course, would not know exactly how your associate sold these pictures.'

'Naturally not. But he was an honest man. He was a friend.' Maurice was puzzled.

'And you and he would work on what—a commission basis?'

'Indeed. That is the most usual.'

'A commission of what? Would it run to forty per cent?'

'That would be unusually high, but there are circumstances . . .' Maurice shrugged.

'Forty per cent commission?' Cohen was astonished. 'That would mean you must be on a heck of a large mark-up.'

Jarvis intervened smoothly before Maurice could take offence. 'And did Ben ever consign pictures to you? Or was the traffic all the one way?'

'Very occasionally he would send to me,' Maurice replied, ignoring Cohen. 'Most usually, it was the other way. After all, in Paris there is too good a supply of pictures. It is less so elsewhere.'

'You mean that the provinces will buy what the expert market discards,' Cohen interjected again, and then subsided at a sharp glance from Jarvis. Maurice continued to ignore him.

'And after the quarrel, you came home here, and were continuing to deal with the Turpin Gallery?' Jarvis asked.

'But yes.'

'Have you been back since?'

'To Glasgow? No, not yet. But we have resumed the business contact.'

'I see,' said Jarvis, rising. 'Well, that is all very helpful. Perhaps we can give you an address and telephone number in case there is anything else you think we should know about. Something may occur to you once we've gone, for I'm sure you're still somewhat stunned at our news.'

'That would be excellent,' replied Maurice, also rising.

Jarvis turned to Cohen, who gave Maurice a card.

'We're staying at the Carnac Hotel, over beside the Eiffel Tower, if you want to get in touch before we leave Paris tomorrow,' added Jarvis. Then he thought of something and sat down again. Maurice also sat. 'I've just got one more question. You've really been most helpful.'

'Yes? What is that?'

'The painting you have outside. The one of Icarus. It reminds me of something.'

Maurice rose to his feet. 'Monsieur, do not play games

with me. You speak of the picture in the Turpin Gallery, do you not?'

'Yes,' conceded Jarvis, not moving from his seat.

Maurice sat down again. 'I suppose you are being what they call *diplomatique*.'

Jarvis gestured assent.

'Well, I will tell you. That painting is the prize of my own Gallery here. We await its recognition. I am sure it is a Delacroix and deserves to be hung in a national museum. But it also struck Ben Turpin. He photographed it. I was amazed to find when visiting him soon after that he himself had attempted a modern pastiche of it. We quarrelled about that too!' Maurice laughed. 'He is no painter.'

'His wife has a better eye?'

Maurice smiled slightly and then nodded briefly. 'As you say.'

'What do you think of Ben's attempt?'

Maurice shrugged. 'No good. It is the wrong style for such a project. But I understand why he tried. I myself essay the sculpture. You will see in my window . . . attempts.'

'Don Quixote?' asked Jarvis.

'At least it is recognizable.' Maurice smiled self-deprecatingly.

Cohen spoke. 'I was noticing that both your picture and Turpin's look as though they were intended to be looked at from below.'

Maurice considered him, then smiled. 'That is right. My picture is definitely intended to be hung high in a room. That is why I suggest that it comes from a château collection, where there would be a number of paintings on display. As in the Louvre. You have seen it? The Delacroix collection?'

'It's a bit small for a Delacroix,' ventured Cohen.

Maurice sniffed.

'So Turpin copied your picture.'

'Copied is not the right word.'

'You know what I mean. Used it as a model.'

'Yes.'

'But Turpin's is no good.'

'I do not like that modern style, all dark lines at the edges and so on.'

'That's what a good many use,' said Cohen.

'Oh, I would not say it's useless. Anything will sell. Look at the streets as you pass.' He indicated his competitors round about.

'These shops look much the same to me,' remarked Jarvis unthinkingly, for something was tugging at the back of his mind.

'I do not know what you mean,' said Maurice stiffly.

'Neither do I,' said Jarvis apologetically as he rose. 'Well, you have been most helpful, and have cleared up a number of matters. Thank you.'

'Thank you,' said Maurice.

'Oh, one thing. I do believe we have actually met before. It had been puzzling me as we talked, but am I not right in thinking that you were at the opening of the new Turpin Gallery last year?'

'Indeed, yes.' Maurice looked puzzled.

'So was I,' said Jarvis. 'I rarely forget a face, and sometimes I remember when and where I saw it.'

Maurice looked quizzically at him. 'I am the same for paintings,' he said. 'But not for people. It is not a useful talent if one forgets the name or the place.'

'Indeed.'

'Do you stay long in Paris?'

'Till tomorrow night.'

Maurice turned back to his desk, took a notelet and wrote on it. He signed it with a flourish. 'If you have time, go to M. Hector's shop in Clignancourt Market. You will see there other, more expensive pictures, of the kind Ben and I sell. You will see that we are not extortionate—we are fair businessmen. I give you this recommendation. Show it to him.'

'What was that about—that at the end?' asked Cohen as they walked away.

'He's watching us go.' Jarvis's voice was quiet. 'See. In that window.' He stopped, appearing to look in the window concerned. Then, as if idly, he turned to look back. Maurice was standing outside the door to his Gallery. Jarvis waved farewell. Maurice responded, a distant figure lifting a hand. Immediately Jarvis remembered the figure in the bookshop doorway in Prince's Square.

They turned the corner.

Jarvis walked on, Cohen tagging along like a faithful hound respecting the obvious need of the other to have silence. Jarvis was lost in thought, badgering his memory. Had Maurice been the man greeted by Imogen Turpin in Prince's Square? If so, why had he denied being recently in Glasgow?

'Well?' asked Cohen at last.

'I want to know whether Maurice has been in Glasgow recently,' said Jarvis abstractedly; then, coming to a halt, he became businesslike. 'Can you get the Air France passenger lists for the last month, say? And particularly for the time of the death and the funeral. Can you find out whether he's made telephone calls to Glasgow? Do the French Telephones now provide listed calls? That'd be useful.'

Cohen was taking notes. When he had finished he put his notebook back in his jacket. 'That's not quite what I meant,' he said quietly. 'I'll go back to Claude-Michel and get on to all that. But it seemed to me you and Maurice suddenly struck sparks.'

'Yes. We did.' Jarvis paused, then prevaricated. 'I reckon he'd not have arranged Ben's death. But I bet there's more to their relationship than he was letting on. You might not be too far off the track in thinking they're fencing Post-Impressionists. Glasgow just might be far enough away from the Continent to be safe. Or safer,' he added hurriedly. 'I'm not questioning the job you're doing.'

Cohen was mollified. 'Yes, I suppose that's true. We don't get circulated with most of the data on missing pictures. There are just too many. It's only the startling thefts that get shunted round all the Forces. Like that altarpiece that we got in photos of the other day.'

'What was that?'

'Somewhere in Germany. Someone had taken a mediæval

altarpiece complete with its pictures. I reckon it was stolen to order. It won't have been stolen to get the insurance ransom.'

'Does that happen?'

'Yes.'

'Indeed. That sounds interesting.'

'And there's that point I was getting at,' said Cohen.

'Yes?'

'I'm willing to bet that a good number of his "minor French Post-Impressionists—"' his tones were mocking— 'are still alive.'

'Mm. I took your point about attribution—and I'm sure he did too,' replied Jarvis.

They walked a few paces in silence, each pursuing different thoughts.

'Why d'you want this stuff checked?' Cohen tapped his pocket. 'You think he has been in Glasgow recently.' The words were statement, not question.

'Yes. I'd swear to it.'

'And he said he hadn't,' said Cohen quietly. 'Well, we'll see what Claude can do for us.'

Jarvis nodded assent. 'But first, you said there was that new Picasso Museum somewhere near here.'

They spent an hour at the Musée Picasso, then went back to see their French police contact who, to Jarvis's surprise, readily agreed to institute the inquiries they wanted.

'Well, that's that,' said Cohen as they left.

'If he comes up with anything,' said Jarvis. 'We'll need to get immigration records as well—no, damn. We don't have records now, do we?'

'Not for EEC nationals. But in any event, if he was back surreptitiously he'd not have travelled under his own name, would he? He'd not have lied if he could be found out that easily.'

They walked along the river bank in the late afternoon sunshine.

'You want to go see that man Maurice recommended?' asked Cohen.

'Not really. What d'you think?'
'Tomorrow, perhaps.'

Later over dinner their conversation turned to the Picasso Museum. Jarvis commented, 'The most striking picture there, apart from that marvellous cat, was the old man at the end. He's such a mixture of bleakness, uncertainty, and yet somehow of a full life.'

'Know what you mean.' Cohen spoke through his duck. 'Reminds me of the Bacon studies and that original, the El Greco of the Cardinal, that Bacon reworked so damned often.'

'You know a lot about art,' observed Jarvis.

'Once I was an art student,' replied Cohen.

'But from what you said you don't like Modern Art.'

'I could do those pastoral scenes by the yard for M. Maurice. Not the recent stuff.'

'So what went wrong.'

'Nothing. It's just not my bag. Listen.'

By the time their meal was over, Jarvis knew much more of his companion, and probably more than Cohen realized.

4

The next day, the Saturday, they breakfasted and separated. Cohen went shopping before meeting Jarvis at Clignancourt. Jarvis himself played the schoolboy, and was at the Eiffel Tower as soon as it opened and before it was infested with tourists.

In the Clignancourt Market they found M. Hector's shop shut. The next-door neighbour indicated M. Hector was gone till the end of the month.

They peered in through the dirty windows, but apart from the fact that there were pictures on display, could see nothing of interest.

'Come on,' said Jarvis to Cohen. 'I know a better place to see pictures. Have you seen the Musée d'Orsay?'

'No. We had to skip it last time. It was just open and the queues were too long.'

At the Musée he found Cohen a knowledgeable commentator on the different periods and styles on display.

'It's difficult to justify this,' observed Cohen as they snacked at the coffee shop on the top floor.

'Not really,' replied Jarvis. 'The only plane back to Glasgow is at six. But if it disturbs you to have some free time, think of it this way. We're dealing with the death of an art dealer who had some sort of speciality in French Post-Impressionists. Makes sense to have a look at some really good ones.'

'That's true,' said Cohen, his mouth full of ham sandwich. 'But why didn't we do it all yesterday and go home then?'

'I don't like working under a deadline. In any case, like I said, we'd have had to check in by five, which would have meant leaving Paris itself by about four—so we couldn't have made it in any case.'

'Good.'

'There's something else here I want to see before we go,' said Jarvis, thumbing through the guide. 'We must have gone past it on our way up. It seems to be at the end of the main floor.'

This 'something else' was the plaster cast of Rodin's Gates of Hell. Jarvis had seen the casting of the Gates that was on display in Washington in 1981, and it had impressed.

'That's quite something,' said Cohen when they found it. 'I'm not much of a one for sculpture, but that's good.'

Jarvis nodded. He went to stand where the Thinker seemed to gaze, and went over the various figures. Then he turned away. The sight of the souls plummeting to Hell reminded him of Ben.

Cohen was keen to spend the rest of their free time shopping—he had not got all he wanted earlier—but Jarvis had been solemnized. Cohen went back to the shops. Jarvis took the Metro along to St Michel, and went into Notre Dame where he sat more than an hour at the crossing of the transepts, watching the passing bustle and every so often raising his eyes to the great purple and blue wheel windows.

He ran over the interview with Maurice, and then reviewed all that had happened, all that he knew. Was there a pattern? But that dragged his thoughts further against his will.

Was Ben's death an accident? That was one question. But there was the general question. Was there meaning to life? Slowly he faced, as he knew he must, the root of that question for him. Why had Patricia died? Was it his fault? Or had it had to happen? He let the pain out, and it washed over him. His side hurt, and he dug out an antacid.

Japanese gentlemen bustled by, popping off flashes in a vain attempt to capture the beauty of the windows. A little old lady remained on her knees before the altar the whole time that Jarvis was there.

Jarvis found himself speculating about her. She was old enough to have gone through the Occupation. What stories lay in her life?

What lay in the lives of any of the passers-by?

He thought of Ben, successful at last—or was he? Cut down by accident in his prime? Or had some past caught up with him? What about the picture and the insurance? How was he to use the insurance?

He thought of Lynn.

He thought of young Ben.

Almost incoherently his thoughts steadied, and he found himself thinking of the piety the Cathedral represented.

'Why, God? Why?'

After a time that transmuted into 'What now?' and he found a measure of peace.

They met again, as appointed, at the Gare du Nord Metro entrance for the train to Charles de Gaulle.

'Cheered you up any?' asked Cohen.

'It helped,' said Jarvis, closing the matter.

5

Back in Glasgow Jarvis refused Mrs Cohen's offer to come home to dinner. He was polite about it. The real reason for refusal was that little things during the two days they had spent together had shown him that Cohen was a good family man. Jarvis just did not want to see what he himself was missing. So he made excuses which Mrs Cohen appeared to accept at their face value, and made his way back to the house provided for him.

There were no letters waiting and nothing on the answering machine, though clearly there had been calls from people who, presumably, were either frightened of or objected to being greeted by a machine. He looked at his notes once more, adding material about the Maurice interview. He circled the word 'Drugs' again on the master sheet, and then put the material aside. He did not feel like reading, there was no music on radio or TV, so he spent the rest of the evening watching a succession of indifferent television and feeling rather lonely before going to bed.

CHAPTER 13

Sunday

Jarvis woke late next morning. He had cancelled the bleeper on his watch, but had expected to wake at his accustomed hour notwithstanding. But it didn't happen. He came suddenly awake, clawing for his watch as on the day he had had that appointment at the Gallery with Imogen Turpin. It was half past nine.

He got up and had his breakfast, listening at first to the morning service on the radio, but the poor man taking the service had almost nothing to say about God, and clearly did not understand economics, so he switched to the concert on Radio Three.

Jarvis expected Sunday to be an easy sort of day even on an investigation. Indeed he contemplated going to church in the morning—it was his usual habit at home—but he had left it too late to get to one of the churches where he knew and approved of the ministry. So he went in to Police Headquarters.

When he entered Cohen's office he found him brimming with excitement.

Cohen looked with exaggerated carefulness at his watch as Jarvis sat down. 'Some of us have been at work for hours,' he said.

'I'm glad to know the citizens are getting value for their money,' replied Jarvis blandly, but with a sufficient twinkle in his eye to rob the remark of offence.

'Well, if you'd been in a bit earlier I'd not have wasted my time and run up the bills phoning you.'

'What's come up?'

'You remember the wire on Turpin's glider was tested for strength and in the classic phrase "found wanting"?'

'Yes.'

'Well, apparently there's something else.' Cohen paused for effect, waited until Jarvis's impatience showed, and continued. 'The bit where the break occurred had been heat-treated, making it even weaker than it already was.' He took a sheet of paper from the pile on his desk and passed it over. 'It came in while we were gallivanting.'

Jarvis got to his feet and went to the window. 'Gallivanting means spending time frivolously,' he said mildly. 'We weren't doing that.'

'Read the thing!' replied Cohen impatiently. 'That's what the previous report meant about further tests. They'd seen something at the fractured bit.'

Jarvis read. He stood there a moment gazing out at the passing traffic, then turned to where Cohen was looking up at him. 'That settles it then. It's murder,' he said coolly and laid the letter back on Cohen's desk.

'It might be suicide.' Cohen's remark surprised Jarvis.

'Logically, but not practically. Ben wouldn't have done that.'

'You're very sure of that?' Cohen leaned back in his chair, his hands behind his head.

'I am. Ben wouldn't destroy himself to get out of something. Not, as it were, voluntarily. Oh, I could see him sacrificing himself for a friend, or even a colleague, if necessary. But not suicide.'

'So he might do that to get rid of his debts. I know there's no insurance, but if they're personal debts, his wife wouldn't be liable. Not in law at least.'

'I can't see Ben killing himself over debts. Besides, we don't know of any.' Jarvis was definite.

'It's still a possibility.'

'No,' said Jarvis, getting tired of Cohen's persistence, and forgetting for the moment the insurance payable to himself. He changed the subject. 'What about this McLintock person? We need to speak to Mr McLintock about those pictures sometime.'

'I've already spoken to him. He's retired down west of Hamilton, and could see us at two. That all right with you?'

Jarvis nodded.

2

Albert McLintock proved to be in his seventies and not entirely fit. He brought the two men into a well-furnished lounge while his wife bustled off to the kitchen intent on producing a cup of tea for the visitors. The lounge was comfortably furnished, its windows looking east over the Clyde valley.

'That's it,' said Mr McLintock, pointing with his stick at a picture to the left of the wooden fireplace. Jarvis crossed to look. It was *The Wheatfield* just as he had seen it in Maurice's polaroid, but it made a better impression when seen full size. He waved Cohen over and spoke to McLintock. 'Very nice. I can see why you bought it.'

'What exactly is the problem?' McLintock inquired. 'Mr Cohen—sorry, Inspector Cohen—was not explicit when he phoned. He just said it was about the picture.'

'We're just checking a few things out,' replied Jarvis smoothly. 'You would have heard that Mr Turpin died?'

'Yes, indeed. It was quite ghastly. Ghastly.' The old man turned and sat down. Jarvis sat beside him.

'There are some matters of police interest arising from

the death. One of them relates to this picture and another which I understand you inspected some time later?' Jarvis trailed the question off.

'Ah yes,' McLintock replied. 'You would be meaning that French gentleman who tried to sell me another.'

Jarvis nodded. 'That's right.'

'There's nothing much to it. Mr Turpin phoned to say he had a colleague who had a picture which he thought might make an interesting pair for *The Wheatfield*, and would I like to see it. He offered to bring it out for me to see. I was a bit reluctant, but he pressed me.'

'May I ask why you were reluctant?'

'My wife was in bed, getting over a dose of 'flu, and I didn't really want visitors. But he had been obliging, so I allowed him to come.'

'So your wife never actually saw the visitors?' asked Cohen.

'No. That's right. She stayed upstairs in bed.' The old man smiled as his wife came in with a tray. 'I was quite discourteous as host, being unable to offer them tea.'

Mrs McLintock put the tray on a table and distributed tea and biscuits.

'I was saying, my dear, that when Mr Turpin and that Frenchman came out about the picture—you remember?—because you were ill I couldn't offer them tea.' He spoke loudly: Mrs McLintock's hearing was clearly imperfect.

'What happened when they were here?' asked Jarvis. 'Did you like the picture?'

'Indeed, yes. But the Frenchman was asking far too high a price for it.'

'Even if you considered the two as a matching pair?'

'Turpin urged that point, but no. It was far too much, even as a pair.' The man spoke slowly and thoughtfully, as if weighing the decision once more.

'Did he offer to purchase *The Wheatfield?*'

'No.' Again the man was thinking. 'Now that you mention it, he did not. Funny. That would be the obvious thing to do, wouldn't it?' He looked from Cohen to Jarvis. 'If he thought it was worth all that much he should have tried to buy my one, shouldn't he?'

'It would seem a sensible alternative,' Jarvis said.

'How did they take your decision?'

'I don't think the Frenchman was all that pleased, but it seemed to make no difference to Mr Turpin.'

'They were on good terms together?'

'Oh yes. It was simply a business project that had fallen through because of the intransigence of an old man.' McLintock laughed.

'But neither was very distressed?'

'No. As I said the Frenchman was a bit crestfallen. Not that he'd any right to be. His price was ridiculously high for pensioners like ourselves. So that was that. More tea?' He motioned his wife into action once more.

'No, thank you,' replied Jarvis getting to his feet. 'Perhaps Mr Cohen could come back and get you to make a formal statement later?' Cohen also stood and nodded at the suggestion.

'Yes. Any time. We like to have visitors and don't get out very much now that I've got this leg.' McLintock had got to his feet and slapped the stick against the right leg. 'It's made driving impossible, worse luck.'

'That doesn't square with Maurice,' observed Cohen as they went to their car.

'Nor with Imogen Turpin,' replied Jarvis.

CHAPTER 14

Monday–Tuesday

Next morning they went for coffee as soon as Jarvis came in. As they drank, Cohen brought them back to the reason for their association.

'None of it seems to have any of the sort of interest that you're here for.'

'I'm quite grateful for that,' replied Jarvis. 'Even so, I want to see it through to an end, one way or the other: accident or . . .' His voice tailed off. He was feeling flat. Either his cold was getting to him, or just the routine business of asking questions and checking was wearing.

Cohen's reply was brisk. 'I'm not sure that Mr McLintock gets us any further. There's nothing there that gives us a motive—the money's too small.'

'Except that what McLintock says is different from Maurice, and from Imogen Turpin.'

Cohen nodded.

'Sir?' The voice belonged to a youngish policeman who was standing in front of their table. He was speaking to Cohen.

'Yes, Charlie?' Cohen turned to introduce the constable to Jarvis, and froze, struggling for the name. 'Charlie's the railway buff I mentioned. Charlie . . . Charlie . . .'

'Munro,' the young man helped him. Jarvis acknowledged him with a nod.

'Yes, Charlie. What's on your mind?' asked Cohen.

'You remember we were talking about things going in threes? About the Turpin widow and her sister.'

'Yes?'

'I've just remembered. The third thing's happened already to the Wintergreens. The eldest sister's husband was electrocuted about four years ago.'

The report to the Procurator Fiscal was brief. Adrian Easson had been trimming an overgrown privet hedge in the grounds of his newly acquired house when he had inadvertently cut into the electric cable.

'I thought these things were supposed to be earthed,' said Cohen, but then grunted as he read on. The equipment had been old and faulty, its insulation perished. The widow had said she had often tried to persuade her husband to get rid of the cutters which had been inherited from the deceased's parents.

The nature of the accident seemed clear enough, and no further police action had been required. The man had been careless and had paid the penalty.

But as he passed the report over to Jarvis, Cohen stabbed his finger at two lines in the middle of the report. Present in the garden at the time of the accident had been the widow, Melanie Easson, Mrs Tessa Bruce and Mr and Mrs Ben Turpin, each of whom had confirmed what had happened.

'Was he insured?' asked Jarvis.

2

By late afternoon they had the answer. They pieced the information together from police files, the lawyer who had acted for the dead man and the local office of the insurance company that had been involved. The biggest help came from two reporters working in the Business section of the major local newspaper, both of whom owed Cohen a favour. These two filled in the background and made it real.

Adrian Easson had been well insured. A self-made businessman in his early forties, he had built a considerable property empire on borrowings from banks, and his three main companies (all private) had had an insurable interest in his business acumen. Each company had insured its managing director, Adrian Easson, for substantial sums. As it happened, the property empire had dissolved after Easson's death. None of his employees had had the same flair as he. And, more fundamentally, the widow and, following the death, sole shareholder did not want to carry on the business. Accountants had been called in and they had liquidated all the businesses to the satisfaction of all parties—except the former employees. The sales of property paid off the sums owed to the bank and to the employees, with just a little left over. The proceeds of the insurances were the remaining assets of the companies which the widow wound up.

'I'm sorry,' said Cohen to Jarvis. 'I'm going to have to

report this. It's getting murky. Just to be safe I'll need permission to widen things.'

'Yes, I suppose so,' agreed Jarvis. 'Will you need me along?'

'Might be best.'

'Right.'

Cohen phoned and arranged an appointment with Superintendent Ingram for early next morning. That done, he put the various files into a shabby holdall. He caught Jarvis's eye. 'It's all right,' he said. 'Against rules, but sometimes helpful. I'm just going to tool through them all in comfort tonight and check I'm not making a fool of myself.'

3

Because of a traffic snarl-up next morning Jarvis was late. He and Cohen had been due in Ingram's office shortly before he eventually arrived. As a result, he and Cohen had no chance to talk before they had to leave for the interview.

'So now you think there's maybe something bigger than just Turpin. Is that what you're telling me?' Superintendent Ingram nodded benignly as he spoke. He seemed detached, like some vast complacent Father Christmas who has heard often before everything the wee boy on his knee is pouring out from his heart. He looked from Cohen to Jarvis and back.

'It seems possible, sir,' replied Cohen.

'And you, for your interest, whatever it is, agree?' Ingram spoke to Jarvis condescendingly.

'I agree.' Jarvis refused to react.

'Well, for what it's worth, you may be right,' said Ingram, getting to his feet. 'But I don't think I agree. You've not really got much to go on. Oh, you can keep an interest running, but it's not a priority from now on.' He saw Cohen's disappointment and waved a quelling hand at him. 'There's lots of other cases about that're more likely to get results. Remember we're trying to get the clear-up rate up,' he explained. 'What you're saying doesn't indicate much chance of a conviction. I'm not saying "drop it". See where it gets to. Keep me in touch. But you remember you've got other things in the in-tray.' He wagged a finger at Cohen.

Cohen and Jarvis got to their feet and were shown out.

'That was short and not so sweet,' remarked Jarvis as they went down the corridor.

'He doesn't waste time,' replied Cohen. 'I see the point he's making. But at least he didn't pull me off the case or cases, whichever it is.'

'Did he OK your going to Paris? Was that the reference to the in-tray? Was he miffed you were away on a jaunt?'

Cohen smiled wryly. 'Yes. He'll not let up for a while yet. And it's true. My in-tray's pretty full.'

'So what now?' Jarvis ignored the last statement. 'I'm beginning to feel that I'm redundant, but I outlined where we were to London and they're willing that I stay on, observing at least. But I don't see I can be much help if he's reducing your hourage on the Wintergreens.'

'We'll see what we can manage. Just don't make too much noise,' Cohen said, smiling. 'Flies on the wall are all very well. It's when they start buzzing that they're a pest.'

'I'll bear that in mind.'

'I've got a grievous bodily harm case to get a statement from. He's in the Royal. They say he'll be able to talk this afternoon, so we've got a little time. Let's keep going on Turpin and the others. Come on to my office. I've been thinking overnight.'

'Right,' said Cohen once they had settled. 'Let's see what we've got. There's three sisters—an elder and twins—who've been singularly unlucky with their husbands. Each husband has died unnaturally. Two were well insured. And there's the possibility that the third wife, Imogen, may have thought that her husband was insured as well.'

Jarvis thought of interrupting to give Cohen the news about the insurance payable to himself, but Cohen was in full flow, ticking off points in the air. There'd be another opportunity.

'You think there's a chance she may have thought her husband was too friendly with the woman next door. So there's three deaths and arguably the widow benefits in each case,' Cohen continued.

'But each could just be bad luck,' said Jarvis drily, following the line of thought. 'You're not going to hang much on that. After all, the widow usually benefits by the death of a husband.'

'"Hang" could be the right word if things were regulated right,' said Cohen, with a frown. 'And in each case . . .' He paused. 'No, I'm wrong. I was going to say the widow was at the scene in each case. It's not like that. But in the first two cases the twins and your friend Turpin were there at the time of the death. In the first two cases the widow was present.'

'Ben was present at the third occasion as well as the others, if you're looking for people in common. But the widow wasn't,' remarked Jarvis.

'So far as we know she wasn't,' replied Cohen. He broke off, gesturing Jarvis, who was about to challenge the statement, to silence. Cohen clenched his teeth. A thought was coming, but eluded him. He turned to another. 'Did you read the statements on the first two deaths?' he asked suddenly.

'Yes.'

'I know you read them.' Cohen was irritated. 'But did you read them together?'

'No. You had the files overnight.'

'True. True. I forgot that.' Cohen got to his feet. 'Tell you what. Take them away and go through them—both sets, and come back and we'll talk.'

Jarvis was puzzled, and showed it. 'I thought you were wanting to review things just now.'

Cohen snorted slightly. 'I was. But there's a reason. Things may be stronger than Ingram's giving us credit for.' He went to the filing cabinet and took out a file and put it on top of the one on his desk. He opened it, took out a couple of sheets of paper and put them in his desk drawer. Then he lifted the files and gave them to Jarvis. 'When you first came on the scene I thought you'd be a right nuisance to have around, but it's not working like that. It's useful to have a non-professional mind to bounce ideas off. It helps.

Here's the Easson and Bruce files. See if you cross-check what I think I saw last night.'

Jarvis accepted the files, but with a raised eyebrow.

Cohen saw it. 'No, no.' He waved a finger. 'I don't mean that as it sounds. You're quite professional in your own way. But it's not the same sort of "professional" that I bump into around these corridors. Now, go away, read and come back. Read it all right through, fast-ish. Don't re-read, and come back soon. In the meantime, there's something else I must get done sharpish.'

Jarvis took his dismissal philosophically, and went off to do what he was told. Cohen wouldn't be asking him to do something for no reason.

He came back in under an hour.

'You took a long time,' Cohen greeted him.

Jarvis took a breath and nodded. 'Tell you what,' he said. He took an index card out of his pocket and flourished it at Cohen. 'This is what I think. You write down what you think, and we'll see.'

'Come on,' said Cohen.

'No,' said Jarvis. 'I've played your game. You play mine. I want to see whether we're talking the same language, not offering you a free opinion that you may or may not have thought of.'

Cohen looked at him. Jarvis put the files down on the desk and waved the card in his face. Cohen pulled a sheet of paper from his drawer and wrote on it. He passed it to Jarvis who handed over the card. Each read what the other had written, and looked solemnly at the other.

Cohen's paper read: 'The stories are too pat.'

Jarvis's card said: 'There is an uncanny similarity in the depositions.'

'That's education for you,' said Cohen.

'I get paid by the word,' said Jarvis with a smile.

'Yes, Minister!' replied Cohen, and then sobered. 'I'm glad you got the same vibes. It's only when you go through the statements fast, as for some reason I did last night, that you see the similarities.'

'I suppose it's possible the likeness between them all is merely because they were each describing more or less the same facts.'

'Yes. I suppose so. But there's something not quite right about it. I used a sheet of paper. Here.' Cohen drew out the two sheets of lined paper he had earlier put in his desk and set them down side by side in front of Jarvis. One was headed 'Easson' and the other 'Bruce'. Each had lines drawn vertically forming columns. Those on the first sheet were headed, *Easson, Bruce, Mrs T* and *T*, and on the second, *Bruce, Mrs T* and *T*. Cohen ran his finger down the first sheet. 'That's the order of the information. There's almost nothing said independently, nothing fresh, and they all follow the same order. It's the same with the other accident.'

Jarvis looked at the sheets. 'I see what you mean.' He picked up a sheet. 'Curious,' he said. 'The last time I saw this sort of thing was in a friend's office. He's a theolog, and it was showing the correspondences between the Synoptic Gospels.'

'The what?'

'The first three New Testament gospels.' Jarvis saw Cohen's expression. 'Sorry! I didn't mean to step on any toes.'

'It's not that. I just didn't know what you meant. Explain.'

'There's books that try to show the relationships between the first three gospels and the order of the events of Jesus's life as each gospel strings the story. The academics say they can deduce things about the gospels from that. But the fourth gospel, John's, tends to take a different line.'

'Oh,' grunted Cohen. 'I don't go in for that sort of thing myself.'

Jarvis stole a look at him, and decided to drop that subject. 'Well, your lists just confirm my—our impression,' he offered as an olive branch. 'There's too much order here. Not enough independent facts or irrelevancies among what they're saying. I'd say there's an agreed story being gone through.'

'Precisely,' said Cohen.

'So where does that leave us?'

Cohen looked down at the papers, and spoke slowly. 'Well—in difficulty. It leaves us a whole lot stronger than I was indicating to Jim Ingram in some ways. But not in others. The Easson electrocution is stale now. The Bruce drowning or whatever's not much better.' He looked up at Jarvis. 'But if your friend's death's part of a pattern, then perhaps we're in business.'

Jarvis sighed. 'And we just don't know that,' he said.

Both men sat down, their minds darting through the possibilities.

'Now if only Turpin had been insured . . .' Cohen said at length, leaning back, his hands behind his head as he stretched.

This was Jarvis's cue. 'I ought to have mentioned this before.' He spoke diffidently.

Cohen stared at him.

'There was an insurance on Ben's life, just like you're wanting. There was a letter waiting for me when I went back north before we went to Paris. I'm the payee.'

Cohen froze.

'It's made payable to me to dispose of as I wish, but there's a request attached that I am to be mindful of widows and children,' Jarvis went on. 'It sounds a weird way to do things, but in Law it's a "discretionary trust". It's a way of keeping the funds involved out of Ben's estate.'

Cohen lowered his hands from behind his head, folded them on the desk in front of him, gazed at them and then quietly stated rather than asked: 'And you've known about this for ten days?'

'Yes.'

'All through our time in Paris?'

'Yes.'

Cohen suddenly rose to his feet and slammed his hand flat on the desk. 'Dammit! How dare you keep something like that from me! It would be bad enough if you were an ordinary member of the public, but from someone in your position that's intolerable! I've a mind to get in touch with your superiors and get you dealt with by them. You realize that that makes you a suspect?'

Jarvis held his hands up. 'Come on! A, I didn't know about the money. B, it's not mine to keep. C, it's not enough to murder for. But I'm sorry. I apologize. It was wrong of me to keep mum. But believe me, it's a great burden—I don't mean not saying anything—I mean trying to decide what I should be doing with the money if it ever does get paid. That's been in my mind too. You see, I knew Ben's first wife well.' He hesitated, then decided to disclose. 'We might have married once, before Ben came on the scene.'

Cohen looked at him, head on one side.

'It doesn't affect my objectivity. But I'm just not sure what to do with the money. I was at dinner with her and her son a week past Monday. And there's the second wife as well,' added Jarvis.

'My heart bleeds for you!' Cohen was gruff.

'It's a real problem.' Quietly.

Something in Jarvis's solemn tone got through to Cohen and he sat down again. He put his hands flat on the desk, thumbs at right angles, tips touching. Then he turned his hands through ninety degrees to make fists. The knuckles whitened.

'Right,' he said. Then he relaxed visibly. 'OK. No real harm done, I suppose, save that you've gone back ten spaces.' He stopped and looked seriously at Jarvis. 'Never again,' he warned.

Jarvis assented.

'Who are the insurers?' asked Cohen, digging into his desk drawer for a pencil.

Jarvis gave the name, and that of the official who had written to him.

'Right.' Cohen threw the pencil back into the drawer and shut it. He leaned back in his chair once more. 'So there was an insurance policy. Someone may have known of it, but not the details, and may have thought it a good enough reason to kill Turpin.' He shook his head, as if to clear it. 'But before we track that, let's go over the other possibilities one more time. What about suicide?'

'You're playing devil's advocate?'

Cohen nodded. 'Why'd'you think it doesn't end up as suicide? It all fits. Perhaps there was another matrimonial crack-up on the way and he couldn't face it. Or more likely in my mind there's something wrong with the business that no one's telling us about, and he thought it was the easy way out.'

'Easy way!' Jarvis's mouth twisted and he came back to a seat near Cohen's desk.

'Say he was slightly off his rocker, then. I'd agree to that.' Cohen shook his head at the thought of suicide by hang-glider. 'Maybe he was also feeling guilty about stealing whatever-her-name-is from you all those years ago and has tried to set you two up for life as some sort of "sorry".'

'Lynn,' supplied Jarvis, getting to his feet and going back to the window. 'And there's not enough money for that. But it still doesn't fit. It's just not the Ben I knew.'

'Cancer?' said Cohen suddenly after half a minute or so had passed. 'How about if he knew there was something nasty wrong with him?'

Jarvis swung round. 'Possible,' he said briskly. 'Where's the . . .' But Cohen was already at his filing cabinet.

The post-mortem report was that Ben Turpin had been in good condition for his age, and had died as a result of multiple fractures to most of the major bones of the torso. He had hit the ground virtually flat. Otherwise the corpse had no apparent health problems.

'I'll phone and ask,' said Cohen. He glanced at Jarvis, then took him by the shoulder. 'Come on, laddie,' he said. 'Get that look out of your eyes. It either is or it isn't. We'll get there yet.'

'There's something else,' said Jarvis in an abstracted tone. 'Lynn—Ben's first wife—when I was at dinner . . . She gave me a picture. She was at Rowardennan round about the right time. Do we know how the glider got up there? Could she have had access to it?'

'We'll check that out,' said Cohen briskly, taking a note. 'Now, getting back to things. There's still the suicide possibility. We haven't got that absolutely ruled out, or have we?'

'I would think the heat treatment of the wire makes suicide a non-starter.'

'I'm not entirely sure about that.' Cohen frowned. 'Maybe he did deliberately put in that weak wire, and then heat treated it to ensure that it would break. Think of it, man!' He stood up for emphasis. 'If you were trying to kill yourself that way, you'd want it to work wouldn't you? You'd not be able to face trying it again.'

'But if that were the case it'd be easier to file the wire thin or something like that. Nick it.'

'That'd be spotted by the Air Accident boys. That'd be sure to cause a fuss. A planned suicide would be wanting everything to run easy, and no questions asked. He'd not risk a question as to the wire being tampered with.'

'All that sounds quite bizarre to me,' replied Jarvis, coming back to the desk and sitting down. 'Too bizarre.'

Cohen sat down as well. 'Agreed. It seems too bizarre to me too. That's why I'm now prepared to swallow your murder theory.'

'My murder theory?'

'You've seemed to think it was murder all along. So it's your murder theory.'

'Thanks,' said Jarvis ruefully. 'Thanks very much.'

He went to the window and looked out. 'As I see it,' he said quietly, 'there is a link between the deaths. I hate to say it, but the first two seem to me to have had Ben as a participant in murder. That's probably where he and Imogen got the money to open their Gallery. Either it was a direct "cut", or the other women are in with them as partners—we'd need to check that out if we can. Ben's own death just might have had the financial element behind it. Or I still think the Andrews woman could be a motive, whether or not there was anything between them. It'd just depend on what Imogen Turpin thought. Or it could just be that the women thought he was a weak link or something.'

Cohen shook his head. His mien showed he dismissed all that Jarvis had said.

'Maybe they were planning to do something he didn't want to do,' added Jarvis.

'Such as?'

'I don't know.' Jarvis paused. 'Unless there was some question of a French connection—a partnership or something with Maurice. I find myself wondering how friendly Maurice is with any of the women. I'm sure I saw him with Imogen Turpin in Prince's Square the day after the funeral when he wasn't supposed to be in Glasgow.' He paused, then carried on. 'Certainly there was something odd about the Bruce drowning, if a Distinction lifesaver goes on record as saying that he couldn't swim.'

'But on the other hand, the Easson death is what—four or five years ago? And the drowning is a couple of years at least. It's all too stale.' Cohen was clearly disappointed at the trend of their thoughts. Elbows on knees, he stared down at his hands held loosely between his knees.

There came a knock at the door. A woman police officer put her head in and said, 'Urgent telex, sir. The number's been traced.' She handed an envelope to Cohen, who opened it and read, As he read he began to chuckle.

'Claude-Michel has sent over some info. Your friend Maurice has been phoning Glasgow.'

'Ah! Turpin Gallery? Imogen Turpin?' Jarvis held out his hand for the sheet of paper.

'No. It's not.' Cohen paused, enjoying the effect. 'It's someone called Easson over on south side. Now where does that put your theory?' He handed over the sheet and opened one of the files. 'It's the right address.'

Jarvis gave it back. 'I wonder if he's phoning Imogen Turpin there. They might set up something like that in case there's a watch on her phone. Or maybe it's the elder sister that's the attraction. Either way the plot thickens. But I haven't a theory. I certainly have a feeling that it must have been more than an accident. If you want a theory I'll go and think about it.'

'Fine,' said Cohen. 'Do that. Meantime I've to get the victim statement from that GBH.'

*

Jarvis went back to Rowardennan and walked up the path as far as the upper edge of the trees. He sat on a rock and stared up at the mountain. It was a warm day, and an ant trail of hikers wound its way up and down. Some midges began to take a proprietary interest in him. He turned and went down to the pier, taking refuge in the cool breeze off the water.

Lynn's picture was a pretty good representation.

CHAPTER 15

Wednesday–Friday

Jarvis drew a breath. 'How fussy are you?' he asked.

Cohen looked up.

'What d'ye mean?'

'I know there are rules about admissibility of evidence and all that, but how fussy are you?' Jarvis emphasized the last word by pointing at Cohen.

'As fussy as I need to be,' replied the other.

Jarvis relaxed. 'In my line of country we're not above the old goat trick.'

'What does that mean? There's a lot of old goats round here.' Cohen smiled.

'Just the old business of staking out a goat to lure the tiger into the open where you can get a clear shot at it.'

'Meaning?'

'Well, I suppose it's not quite that, but how would it be if I blunder about a bit and say some stupid things? I might manage to knock something free. Act the goat, as it were. As a private individual—nothing official.' His voice slowed as he saw Cohen's expression.

Cohen sat silent, looking at him.

'Look. The only thing that fits logically is that Imogen is involved—with or without outside help. I think I can get some way towards establishing that if I have a go myself,' said Jarvis earnestly. 'I'd prefer to do it with your approval. If we can break Imogen, then perhaps she may give something on the other deaths.'

Cohen sat.

'It's not that daft,' said Jarvis. 'I have done it before.'

'Have you now?' Cohen's reply was slow. 'Well, that just might be interesting.' He shifted in his chair.

'I expect it'd be quite against your normal procedures—and maybe nothing I'd turn up could be used in court, but if we're going to get anywhere it seems the best way to me. It might give us somewhere to attack under the formal rules.'

Cohen got to his feet. 'I'm having nothing to do with that. It's not for a serving officer to encourage irregularities in police work.' His voice was harsh. Then he smiled and pointed to the door, his thumb, first finger and clenched fingers pistol-like. He mimed a shot.

Jarvis took the hint. 'I'm going for a quiet walk down beside the river. I might do some thinking out loud,' he said, also rising. 'You know, if I were engaged on a private enterprise with no police encouragement or backing, or better—assuming that we're talking now entirely hypothetically . . . ?' He raised an eyebrow.

'You're right. It is a nice day for a walk,' replied Cohen calmly. 'In fact, it'd be a pity to waste it.' His spirits were rising, Jarvis thought.

'A pity? A crime, perhaps?' Jarvis felt a surge of adrenalin. His hobbles were dropping off. The need to cooperate with Cohen, or at least to carry him with him, had been a drag. He'd be freer acting on his own—but maybe Cohen might see a wrinkle—or pitfalls—on his intentions for the next few days.

The two of them left the office.

2

After lunch Jarvis phoned the Turpin Gallery.

'Turpin Gallery. How may I help you?' came Imogen Turpin's voice.

'Sorry. Wrong number,' replied Jarvis in guttural Glaswegian, and hung up.

3

'Go away,' said Mrs Andrews, making to shut the door when she saw who stood on her doorstep. 'I've got nothing to say to you!'

Jarvis stopped the door with his foot and raised placating hands. 'Look, I'm sorry,' he said. 'I got things wrong. I was thinking more of my friend Ben as I used to know him than of you.'

She hesitated, taking the pressure off the door.

'It's just that I desperately want to clear up why he died. We were good friends in past years,' pleaded Jarvis.

She let the door open a little.

'I admit I made a mistake. I wasn't thinking. I was blundering on on a particular train of thought when we spoke last.'

'Hm.' She paused. 'All right. But if you offend again I'll have a complaint in to the Chief Constable before you know what's hit you.'

'Fair enough.'

They went once more to her lounge. The flowers in the window had been changed, but were still gorgeous. She noticed his appreciative reaction to them and appeared a little mollified.

'Well?' Her tone was guarded, but not hostile.

'I was wondering if—if you spend as much time in your garden as you indicated you did—if you happened to see Ben Turpin working on his glider in his garage, over summer?'

She paused to think. 'I can't actually say I do remember that. In fact, I don't think he did any work on it. It was Mrs Turpin who used to be in and out, pottering about.'

'Did Mr Turpin not have evenings when he was there with other glider people, swapping yarns and doing work on their gliders? Sort of partying?'

'Not really. I remember one evening back in early summer when there were a few people over. That got quite noisy. He had a barrel. My husband went over as well, and it was quite a night. But that's the only partying so far as I can remember.'

'Did you see Mr Turpin doing work on the glider in, say, the last month?'

She shook her head. 'I saw Mrs Turpin checking the thing out.' She paused. 'She had some help in, I remember. A thin man.'

'You mean Mrs Turpin looked after the glider?'

'That was my impression.'

'That's not what everyone thought. Mr Turpin did his own repairs.'

She smiled. 'Many wives let their men think they do the work—or allow them to take the credit.'

Jarvis spent the evening again with his sheets of paper.

In the morning, Jarvis made a couple of phone calls, booked a return flight to Paris for two days ahead and finally phoned Cohen.

'His doctor? What for? I checked the post-mortem report and there was nothing there.'

'Even so, I've had an idea.'

'Just a minute.'

Jarvis heard him go to the filing cabinet and rummage, then Cohen came back with a name and an address. 'Going to tell me what it's all about?'

'No. Better not. We agreed that anything I got up to was nothing to do with you.'

'Fine. But . . .'

''Bye. I'll be in touch.'

For his age, Turpin had been in excellent condition.

'Just like you say, Mr Jarvis,' continued the doctor, 'his only blemish was his eyes.'

4

From the doctor Jarvis went back out to the Campsie Hang-Gliding Club.

'Could you repeat for me the standard procedure before a flight?' he asked. 'Just go over it, if there is a check-list.'

The Secretary ran through pre-flight procedures.

'So let me get this straight,' said Jarvis finally. 'Anyone going up on one of these things would have checked the equipment before setting off.'

'Of course. That's why there's the standard list we run through. It makes sure that everything is checked—that nothing's missed.'

'But you wouldn't have known whether Ben Turpin went through that procedure or no.'

'Well, I wasn't there, of course. His wife usually did it for him, but he was usually all right in going over things when he did it himself. Not perhaps everything. He'd often just twang the wires and so on. But that'd do. Only a fool wouldn't check their tautness, and Ben Turpin wasn't a fool—not where safety was concerned, at least.' The man smiled.

'That's the Ben I remember.' Jarvis smiled back. 'But none the less something went wrong.'

'Yes. A tragedy, that. But if there was some hidden weakness, I suppose it wouldn't be noticed.'

'A weak wire, for example.'

'Just so. You can't tell strength by sound.'

'But why wouldn't it have been spotted earlier? He'd been up recently?'

'It'd be a matter of gravities. From what I remember, he turned to make a left against the wind. There'd be an updraught on the hillside. That could put the total weight above what the wire could stand. It hadn't been under that strain before. When it went over—pfft!' The Secretary shrugged.

5

In the early afternoon, Jarvis went to see Turpin's accountant once more. He had nothing to report. As far as he was concerned, his connection with Turpin had ended with the death, and he was simply finalizing accounts as far as he knew them for the lawyer who was handling the estate.

Later in the afternoon he went back to see Turpin's lawyer. Remembering what Cohen had said about the man's dislike of policemen, Jarvis was anxious as to the best line of approach. He felt there must be a way. And surely the man had cause if he held the police responsible for his child's death and the bungled trial of her killer. Even if the first was irrational, there were good grounds in the second.

But he need not have worried. The slight warmth Jarvis had detected at their parting seemed to have persisted.

Jarvis was moved to comment, 'You seem more comfortable to see me alone than with my police colleague.'

The man smiled wanly. 'Ah! You see, I knew there was something—that you weren't quite a real policeman, whatever your role is. But it's a good day in general. I've just pulled off a very good deal.' To Jarvis's surprise, however, he seemed drained rather than elated.

'Congratulations,' offered Jarvis, unsure what else could be said.

The lawyer's smile became slightly less formal. 'Yes. I suppose congratulations are in order.' He sighed. 'It's been a difficult three weeks, but we've got through and pulled it off.'

'I've been having a difficult time too,' remarked Jarvis.

The lawyer looked at him and nodded. 'I dare say.'

'I believe you've nearly finished winding up Ben's estate?'

'Yes. There's not much actually to be done now. His accountant has passed us an almost complete set of accounts for the year to April, and our own men have dealt with things after that.'

'The paperwork from the Gallery is adequate?'

'It'll do for our purposes. It turns out to be fairly simple.

A good deal of the business is in fact dealt with in Mrs Turpin's name and her accounts. Mr Turpin seems latterly to have not had much to do with that side of things. That means it doesn't enter into his estate for our purposes.'

Jarvis paused: this information resonated. Then: 'Ben Turpin was a good friend of mine. We were at University and then in work together.'

'You mentioned something to that effect.'

'That's why his death puzzles me. Puzzles me extremely. He was a careless sod, but not when it was a matter of his own safety.'

'That sounds intriguing,' replied the lawyer. 'You were in a few ... difficult situations together?'

'If I wanted to be melodramatic about it, I would say he literally saved my life.' Jarvis laughed lightly, and shrugged. 'But it wouldn't be true. But we did watch each other's backs. That sort of thing gives you a fellow feeling.'

'I know what you mean.' The lawyer spoke quietly—as though a memory had obtruded.

'Then to see him falling out of the sky ... that was a great shock.'

'It must have been. I didn't see it.'

Jarvis got to his feet, and paced about for a few seconds in thought. The lawyer watched impassively.

'Can I speak off the record?' asked Jarvis.

'Feel free. If it will help.'

'The fact is that there is a reasonable suspicion that Ben's glider was tampered with. And I want to find out who did it.' He sat down again.

'Indeed.' The lawyer was blank-faced.

'I know all the business about professional privilege and all that. I have the distinct impression that, although Ben was your client, you didn't care much for him. But I wonder whether despite all that—and quite off the record—you could help me. I mean quite off the record. I—we'd—find other ways of getting to the truth that'd not involve you. It's just that it's important to clear these things up if at all possible. I believe in retribution,' he finished with a rush.

There was a long silence. Then: 'So do I,' came the reply.

'Can you help me?' Jarvis asked after an interval.

'No. Not voluntarily.'

The reply shook Jarvis. There was a pause as he considered his next words. The lawyer broke the silence.

'But that is because I do not know what you want to know.'

'Could I just speculate—brainstorm? Let the thoughts roll?'

'Do.'

Jarvis marshalled his thoughts briefly, then spoke to the floor, his head in his hands. 'First, I wonder what happened last year. Why Ben suddenly made that will.'

'I don't know. He just phoned up, came in and made it.'

'Had he a prior will?'

'Not that I know of.'

Jarvis paused. Then: 'Second, I find myself wondering about matters back before last year. I wonder where Ben got the money from for that Gallery.'

'Some from his sister-in-law Melanie Easson. A good deal more from the other sister-in-law, Tessa Bruce.'

'Might there be documents in the matter?'

'There is no partnership agreement, but I dare say it would be possible to trace bank transactions.'

'What about his own funding.'

'Very little. There are some from his wife.'

'Both Bruce and Easson died accidentally.'

'True.'

'Which may be the source of that funding.'

There was no reply to this. Jarvis looked up. The lawyer had swivelled his chair and was facing a wall of books.

'Ben was present at both the Easson and Bruce deaths,' Jarvis continued.

'I didn't know about his being present at the Easson death. But that fits. I wasn't happy with their involvement with the Bruce death,' the lawyer volunteered. 'But don't quote me.'

'But if you suspected something, shouldn't you have told the police?'

'I knew nothing. Besides, who am I to tell the police how to do their business?' The tone was bitter.

Jarvis ignored it. 'I find myself wondering whether Imogen Turpin thought that Ben was insured too.'

'She did.' The voice was soft, and it did not immediately register with Jarvis.

'Because if she did, then maybe . . . what did you say?'

The lawyer turned to face Jarvis. 'She did. She sat in that chair you're in and defied me when I said there was no insurance policy payable.'

'She told me that Ben had refused to extend his insurance to cover the gliding.'

The lawyer gave a bitter laugh. 'It was I that told her, after the death, that the rather large insurances on Ben Turpin were not payable because he had died while engaged in a dangerous sport.'

'Did she accept what you said?'

'I don't know. She may have written to the insurance companies on the matter. She said she was going to.'

Jarvis let out a long sigh—that was checkable data. 'There's just one more thing.'

'Yes?'

'How were they getting on—I mean matrimonially? Were there any rumours, or incipient splits, or anything?'

'Not that I heard of. But then I don't usually hear from my clients on such things until one or other comes in demanding a divorce.'

Jarvis turned the conversation to generalities, and eased his way out.

'Thank you,' he said as they parted.

'You hit the right button,' replied the lawyer.

'Button?'

'Retribution.' The lawyer paused. 'You wouldn't know what I mean, but today would have been my daughter's twenty-first birthday. The day I pull off my biggest deal is the flattest in my life. Goodbye.' He walked back along the corridor to his office, leaving Jarvis to find his own way out.

6

On the Friday Paris was still warm.

'I have done some checking since we spoke when you were here,' said the French detective, Claude-Michel Amiel. 'I regret that there is little that I can give to help other than the matter of the phone calls that I sent to M. Cohen. The Air France flights to Glasgow information has also been given me for the last two months, but it does not appear that M. Maurice made use of those flights. Nor was he on flights to London in the time. But it occurs to me that perhaps he went by British Airways or some other of your carriers? You could check that?'

Jarvis kept himself from disappointment: after all, he could hardly expect that Maurice would use his own name if in Glasgow 'unofficially'. He explained this to Claude-Michel.

'Yes. That is true. But you will, of course, check the British Airways?'

'Naturally. But I don't think that'll help.'

There was a pause, while the two looked speculatively at each other.

'I can understand why you are concerned to avenge the death of a friend,' mused Claude-Michel. 'I cannot think, however, that there is any possibility from here, unless . . . ?'

'Yes?' Jarvis found the Frenchman's tone encouraging.

'Sometimes it can help to make the attack direct.'

'You mean, ask him?'

'Perhaps. I was thinking, however, of something not quite as direct as that—not at first. If we could establish that he was not in Paris at the time through, say, his appointment book or something of that nature . . . ?'

'Mm! Then we could check where he said he was supposed to be.'

'But we must do so in such a way that he is not able to warn the people he says he was with before we see them.' Claude-Michel stood. 'I think we shall go and lunch. Immediately. Then about half past the one o'clock we shall visit M. Maurice's establishment. With luck the receptionist will be willing to speak with us.'

It was the same receptionist that Jarvis and Cohen had encountered. When she asked how she might assist them, Claude-Michel swept his hat from his head, bowed, and spoke rather too rapidly for Jarvis's comfort. But it seemed to work, and she took them through to her tiny office.

'Messieurs?' she asked, once the door was closed.

Jarvis was nervous. 'When will M. Maurice return?'

The woman shrugged. 'He never returns before three.' It was 1.45.

Claude-Michel smoothly took up the conversation. He asked her how she found Maurice as an employer. She sighed and rolled her eyes to the ceiling. M. Maurice was demanding.

Did he pay a good salary?

She laughed bitterly. But it was a start into art.

Did she plan to stay long with M. Maurice?

She did not. As soon as she could find another job, perhaps with more money, she would be off. He treated her as a mere secretary, whereas she had a Diploma in Fine Art. She had to type letters, while she was trained to classify and value.

Claude-Michel sympathized, then briefly showed her his identification. She was interested. Were the gentlemen here on official business? She had had doubts occasionally . . .

Jarvis relaxed.

They were, in fact, making some official inquiries, Claude-Michel continued. They were seeking to establish where M. Maurice had been between certain dates and hoped she might be able to help them.

That was no problem. She kept the Appointments Diary.

M. Maurice was busy? Many appointments?

Yes. He saw many people. His Diary was an essential part of business. What were the dates?

Claude-Michel gave them.

She looked up the Diary, shut it, and asked to see Claude-Michel's identification again. This time she took the plastic folder, read its contents and compared the photograph with the person.

Then she spoke: 'On those dates M. Maurice was away. The Diary indicates he was in Geneva, at the salerooms there. I know that he was not. Usually I book his hotel in Geneva—he goes there frequently. But not that time. Instead I received a call to tell him that M. Martin was booked in to the Burnside Towers, Glasgow. I remember when I told him the message, he smiled.'

'You were puzzled?' asked Claude-Michel.

'Yes.'

'Did M. Maurice go often to Glasgow?'

'Occasionally. There was an association—a business contact he was developing—some small dealer or other. He takes items we find difficult to sell here.'

'His name was Martin?'

'No. It is M. Turpin.'

'So was M. Maurice starting another association with a M. Martin there?'

'I think not.' The girl's voice was decided. 'It was a woman who gave me the message. I felt that the booking was for M. Maurice.' She shrugged expressively.

'Do you know if he is going back to Glasgow in the near future?' asked Jarvis.

She opened the Diary. 'Next week. Wednesday,' was the short reply.

They left. As they did so, Claude-Michel gestured at the sculptures in the window. 'He asks money for that?' He was incredulous.

'Quite a lot of money too, I believe,' replied Jarvis. Then a thought crossed his mind. He stopped. 'I wonder if there's something else you could find out for me.' He explained.

'How quixotic,' laughed Claude-Michel Amiel.

'I wonder whether she was so forthcoming precisely because it was a woman who passed the message about the hotel booking?' mused Jarvis later.

Claude-Michel smiled. 'What is it you say? A woman scorned?'

'A woman scorned can be very helpful,' replied Jarvis.

'To others!'

'I wonder whether M. Martin went on an Air France flight,' Jarvis wondered aloud.

'If he was careless. Come. We shall see,' was the enthusiastic reply. 'And there is something else. If he was in Glasgow you would wish to check. You will need to be able to show a picture. I will try to arrange that we have a photograph of him taken—unseen, of course.'

'Unseen?'

'I forgot. Unobtrusive, perhaps?'

'Yes. That'd be very helpful. A specimen of his handwriting, or his signature would be useful too.' Jarvis stopped. 'No. I have that already.'

'Indeed. Such forethought!'

CHAPTER 16

Saturday–Sunday

A day trip to Paris was not a good idea, Jarvis thought as he woke late next morning. He had had to get up too early the previous morning and two flights and the busy few hours in between had been a bit much. He hadn't got sufficiently over that fluey cold before tackling a day like that. Nonetheless, he told himself in the mirror as he shaved, progress had been made. It might have been worth it.

It was eleven o'clock as Jarvis entered the police headquarters, and Cohen took him down to the canteen for coffee.

'How goes it?' asked Cohen as he brought the coffee over.

'Not too bad. But I'd better not tell you what's going on until there's something concrete to say. Except one thing. You may be getting a data across from Paris. It's for me.'

Cohen was surprised. 'Paris!'

Jarvis did not enlighten him.

'So I'm a post-box now,' Cohen grumbled goodnaturedly.

'How's things at this end?' Jarvis asked.

Cohen shrugged.

Jarvis was not sure whether this meant there was nothing, or whether Cohen was merely repaying his own unwillingness to talk. He did not want to make an issue of it, however. That might just jeopardize his own freedom of action, so he turned to generalities.

They were on their way back to Cohen's office when Jarvis saw two detectives escorting a woman pass on the landing one floor below. The woman was Lynn Redpath. She looked up at him, then quickly looked away.

'Just a minute!' Jarvis caught Cohen by the elbow and pulled him round to face him. 'What's she doing here?' He pointed to the disappearing figures below.

He read Cohen's eyes swiftly. 'What've you been doing behind my back?' he shouted at Cohen.

Cohen shook himself free. 'We're not needing to talk in the stair.' He turned and went upstairs two at a time and along the corridor to his own room. Jarvis followed, fuming.

Once inside, Cohen gave an irritated sigh, then spoke before Jarvis had marshalled his own thoughts. 'Look, I'm sorry you had to find out that way. But it seems to me from various things, including what you've said yourself, that Mrs First Wife can't be excluded from the investigation as easily as you're doing. So we went to see her. Yesterday. And what d'ye think we found? She was working at a table with a small butane torch.'

'So? She used to work with glass. When I saw her she said she was thinking of taking it up again. She's obviously done just that.'

'A butane torch? A small portable butane torch.' Cohen spaced the words out.

'Oh, come on!' Jarvis was exasperated. 'You mean she heated the faulty wire? That's not on. Lynn'd never do something like that.' He turned in disgust.

'Look, laddie,' said Cohen gently. 'I said I'm sorry. But

I've a job to do. She's just in to make a statement. That's all—at present.'

'At present?' Jarvis was incredulous.

'At present.' Cohen's voice was heavy. 'Look. You're not a real policeman. Let me do my job.'

'Job!' Jarvis snorted.

Cohen was starting to lose his temper. 'We've got someone tampering with the glider by heating the wire. We've got someone who on your own evidence—remember that picture she gave you—was up in the area when the glider was unattended. And she's got a very portable car torch—just the kind of thing that'd be needed on a hillside in the dark.'

Jarvis pursed his lips, about to speak, but Cohen resumed. 'And there's other problems.' Cohen's voice went quiet with the last words, and he waited while Jarvis got control of himself.

Jarvis walked to the window. He saw his face in the glass and blanked his expression. He breathed deeply. Then he turned back and looked at Cohen with narrowed eyes. 'You're instructed to keep me informed of whatever goes on, and accept my instructions should I choose to give them.' His finger stabbed out, emphasizing his words.

'Yes. That's true. But if you think that requires me not to investigate matters that require investigation, or indeed to inform you when . . . when . . .' Cohen paused, then started again. 'If you'd just think straight for a second or so, you'd see that there's too big a connection with yourself. At the very least an observer might say your judgement could be rocky. You and she were very close, weren't you? And what about that insurance?' Cohen was now brisk and businesslike. 'Well?'

Jarvis came back to Cohen. He was tempted to hit him, realized that his fists were clenched and deliberately relaxed them. Some unconnected part of his own mind suddenly came forward and pointed out that Cohen was developing a pimple at the side of his nose. Jarvis relaxed, letting out a deep sigh. 'Yes. All right. I see why you did it. Now—fill me in.'

Cohen put an avuncular hand on his shoulder. 'That's

better, laddie. That's better,' he said. He went and sat behind his desk. 'I'll tell you the rest later, if necessary. I may as well say—for you'll find out—that I did think it necessary to check your own movements around the accident dates.' He held up a hand to stop Jarvis's reaction to his words, and carried on. 'It's all right. You're in the clear. Now, how about you filling me in on what you've been doing before we get on to Mrs Redpath? Or can she wait?'

Jarvis shook his head slowly. 'I'm not ready to discuss what I've been doing. Not yet. First, could I have a look at all the files and statements you've got, including the reporters up the mountain? Lynn can wait till later if you're not actually charging her.'

Cohen waved a hand towards his filing cabinets. 'Feel free.'

Jarvis used the desk at the side of Cohen's room. He laid out the files on top of what was already there, took off his jacket, and started. He took occasional notes on a pad he borrowed from Cohen. He paused for a sandwich mid-afternoon, when a pain in his side reminded him that he was supposed to eat regularly.

'I'm off,' said Cohen about half past four. 'Take the files home if you like, but I'll need them tomorrow.'

'Isn't that against regulations?'

'You can use my old holdall. It's under the table.'

They left the building together.

2

On Sunday Jarvis went to church. Twice.

In the evening, after church, he took out the pictures once more and arranged them against the settee.

3

On Monday morning Cohen slid a report over his desk to Jarvis. 'I think you'd like to see this.'

Jarvis read it. It was from a metallurgic analyst confirming that two samples of wire were from the same roll. He passed it back to Cohen with an impassive face.

Cohen made to put it back into a file, so Jarvis leant forward and put his hand on the file. 'Come on,' he said. 'Time to 'fess up.'

Cohen smiled. 'Remember I was interested in the wire fence between the Turpins and that sleek woman next door?'

Jarvis nodded. He could see what was coming.

'It's the same wire as was on the glider.'

'Well,' said Jarvis sitting down. 'In that case I suggest that you and I should put our cards together. I think we may have a full house.'

4

The rest of Monday, Tuesday and much of Wednesday was spent checking. On Wednesday a telex came in from Paris from Claude-Michel Amiel. He confirmed that Maurice was a competent worker in wire, but regretted a thousand times that he had been unable to get a photograph taken of M. Maurice. The services of the divisional photographer had been required at another event.

On Wednesday evening when the Paris plane arrived just after seven in the evening, Cohen and Jarvis watched Maurice come through Passport Control and Customs. As Maurice left Customs Imogen Turpin threw herself into his arms. The man quickly disentangled himself, obviously objecting to her enthusiasm in a public place, and the two of them left the terminal.

Cohen and Jarvis let them go, for they had arranged for them to be followed. In the meantime they went back to headquarters and waited while the police photographer's efforts were developed. Inside half an hour they had three good prints one of Maurice full-figure and two face, one full and one profile. Armed with these, Cohen and Jarvis went to the Burnside Towers Hotel. The receptionist recognized Maurice's photograph, and the registration details in Mr Martin's name were written by the same hand as Maurice's recommendation to the man in Cligancourt Market.

5

At six the following morning Cohen and Jarvis drove out of Glasgow.

'I've just got a slight nagging feeling,' said Jarvis as they turned into the road leading to Buena Vista.

'Why?' replied Cohen pulling the car about on the twisting road. 'It checks. They're in cahoots together. Maurice has spent the night there. He works with wire in his sculpturing. The wire's the same as the fencing wire. Maurice was in Glasgow when Turpin died, though he denied that to us. The Andrews woman saw the two of them at the glider. You've shown me that Turpin couldn't have done the checks on his equipment well enough because he couldn't see close up. He'd not have noticed a different wire. So long as it twanged that'd be all right for him. His fight with Maurice happened all right, the hospital records show Turpin was treated for a cut above the eye, but the reason was Imogen, not that stupid picture. She thought Turpin was insured. What more d'you want? Jam on it? We'll just turn up on the doorstep now and grill the pair of them. I reckon the shock'll shake her at least enough to get us into court.'

Jarvis sighed. 'Yes, but.'

'But what?'

'But it doesn't feel right.'

'Feel!' Cohen was incredulous as he pulled the car round a bend. 'Feel!' He snorted.

Some minutes later they rang the bell of Buena Vista.

Jarvis had often wondered what the precise circumstances were in which one might say someone blenched. His curiosity was satisfied when Imogen Turpin with a wrap round her, opened the door.

Inside they took her into the lounge and sat her down.

'Who's there?' said a man's voice, and Maurice came into the room wrapping a dressing-gown round himself. He stopped abruptly on seeing Cohen and Jarvis.

They stood looking at him.

Imogen Turpin buried her face in her hands.

'What is this?' began Maurice.

'I am here in connection with the unlawful killing of Ben Turpin,' stated Cohen.

'It's not true!' Imogen Turpin's voice was quiet, and then she repeated herself forcefully and got up from her chair. Cohen moved to stop her, and Maurice hit him.

'Wait! Wait!,' she screamed at Maurice, pushing him away. She whirled on Cohen. 'I've got something you ought to see before you go any further.' She turned to Jarvis. 'Can I go and get it?' she asked him.

He spread his hands and nodded. The woman left the room.

She was not gone long. She gave a bundle of letters to Cohen, went to Maurice who was sitting in a chair, and sat on the floor beside him.

The letters were held together by an elastic band. They were on different coloured notepaper. Some were in envelopes also of various colours. Cohen took them over to the window and gave Jarvis about half. His mouth turned down as he handed them over. 'Your hunch?' he said.

The bundle that Jarvis had were largely undated, but those that were two to one year old. They were, to put it mildly, passionate. Most were unsigned. Those that were were signed 'E' in a circle.

Jarvis finished looking through his bundle and waited.

Cohen handed him one from his bundle that he had already read. It was a declaration of hate, also signed 'E'.

Cohen watched Jarvis read it, sighed and turned to Imogen Turpin who sat erect, almost proud, on the floor.

'This was what the burglar was after?' he asked quietly.

'I expect so.'

'Where were they?'

'He kept them in the rafters beside the hot tank behind the spare bedroom wall.'

'That's why you weren't too upset at the burglary. You'd checked they were still safe.'

She shrugged.

Cohen shook his head in disbelief. 'Why didn't you show

them to me before? If you knew that was what they were after why didn't you say?' His voice was calm, but had an edge to it.

The woman shrugged again and snuggled closer to Maurice's legs. He put his hand on her cheek, and she covered it with her own.

Cohen gave a slight bow to the pair. 'I'll need to consider this further. In the meantime I would be grateful if you, Mr Maurice, did not leave Glasgow, and if you would both keep me informed as to your movements.'

'Of course,' she said in a low voice. Then she got to her feet and came to Jarvis. 'I did love him,' she said earnestly. 'But he went away from me.'

He nodded.

'You said you knew him well. So you would understand.'

He nodded again and stared at her. She shifted uneasily under his gaze.

'So what it comes down to is this,' he said slowly. 'You were willing that there should be a mystery. But if it came to a choice between her and you, you vote you.'

She raised her head and stared back. 'Wouldn't you?'

CHAPTER 17

Trial

Jarvis came down for the end of the trial. As the date got nearer he felt he could not face sitting through the evidence. And once the trial was on he found he avoided the newspaper accounts. But he wanted to be there for the end, and was there for the judge's summing up. As he entered the public gallery, Jarvis saw Lynn and Ben Turpin sitting at one side, accompanied by a middle-aged man. With a sinking feeling, Jarvis deduced he was a minder from one of the tabloids.

He sat at the other end, and listened. He thought the judge was fair. Perhaps too fair. His Lordship summarized the evidence, the correspondence, the witnesses Cohen had found to speak to the relationship between the accused and Turpin, including the hang-gliding club secretary who had believed her to be Turpin's wife. Then there was her Army training, the wire in her garage, her proven mechanical competence, her own statements under Cohen's questioning and her evidence, for she had chosen to give evidence. Was all that a complete picture? Much of what had been spoken of was individually innocent in criminal terms. The jury would have to make their minds up. But finally there was the odd point that the accused had asked the officers searching her garage if they thought she had heated the bloody wire. That the wire had been so sabotaged was known only to a few and had not been mentioned to her.

Emma Andrews sat impassive in the dock, well-dressed and attractive. It was hard to believe her guilty.

'God. Let justice be done,' Jarvis prayed fervently.

Most of the public left as the jury retired, but Jarvis sat on. He didn't want to see or speak to anyone. But after two hours he began to think of a coffee. However, he was scared to go in search of one lest the jury should return while he was absent. Quarter of an hour later the gallery filled. The jury had made up their minds.

It was a majority verdict.

As she turned to go below to begin her sentence, Emma Andrews caught sight of Jarvis sitting in the public gallery. Her glare was basilisk. It was the same expression she had thrown at Cohen and Jarvis after she asked if she was suspected of heating the wire. It had suddenly gone quiet, and as Cohen asked her to repeat herself she had realized what she had said.

She tossed her head and disappeared from view.

Jarvis moved into the public corridor. Cohen was waiting for him.

'I saw you up there,' he said.

Jarvis sighed. 'I felt I had to come.'

'I know. I must say I thought we'd blown it, but then

she elected to give evidence and Crown Counsel blew her apart.'

'So that was it,' said Jarvis. 'I wondered. The summing up seemed to go the other way.'

'Yeah. But if you'd seen her yesterday on the stand you'd have had no doubt. She wouldn't take her counsel's advice. Remember I said her signature indicated a strong woman? Self-opinionated. She'll have a few years to regret that.'

'What about her husband?'

'They took him out the other way. They'll give them a few minutes together, though what he'll be saying I couldn't guess.'

Jarvis shook his head quietly. 'Well, I'm glad you didn't need me to give evidence. It's just as well Charlie Munro was there also to corroborate her question.'

Cohen smiled. 'It might have been difficult to explain your presence.'

Beyond Cohen's shoulder Jarvis caught sight of Lynn Redpath and her son Ben coming from the other door into the court. They were escorted by the same middle-aged man.

She spoke to the man, and then came across to where Jarvis and Cohen stood, leaving her son with the man.

She held out her hand and Jarvis took it.

'Thanks,' she said quietly.

He said nothing, but smiled, his head slightly on one side.

'Can I ask you a question?'

'Mm.'

'I've had a letter from Ben's lawyer. It seems someone's set up a trust to pay for young Ben's education. It'll even help with University.'

'Mm?'

'I was wondering if that was you?'

Cohen stared into space.

'Whatever makes you think I've got the wherewithal to do something like that?' replied Jarvis.

She sighed with obvious relief. 'I want you to meet

someone,' she said. 'If you would excuse us a moment—' this to Cohen, who gestured agreement.

She took Jarvis back to where the man and boy stood.

'I'd like you to meet Andrew Clark.' The two men shook hands. Jarvis saw a man in his early fifties, slightly balding, with a worn shirt-collar.

'We're engaged,' said Lynn. 'Andrew's a widower, and we've taught together for . . . is it two years now?' She turned to the man for assistance.

'Bit over that, my dear,' he said affably.

'Peter was a colleague of . . . of Ben's. He knew us when we were married. You were at the wedding, weren't you?' This time she turned to Jarvis for help.

He saw the plea in her eyes. A clinical part of his mind also recognized, as he had before, the determination of a practical woman, but he shrugged that aside. Here, perhaps, lay safety, comfort and companionship for someone who had been lonely and wounded. He knew the feeling, the attraction, the lure. And he hadn't the heart to challenge or even in the mildest way to disturb her decision. Her son too would benefit. Rather than lie, he ignored her question.

'Good for you,' he said quietly. 'Be blessed.' And he bent and kissed her cheek.

'We'd better be going, hadn't we?' the man suggested gently, putting his hand on her arm. She turned to him.

'Goodbye, Ben,' said Jarvis, holding out his hand to the youngster. 'Perhaps we'll meet again sometime.'

'Thank you, sir. I'd like that,' said the boy. Then the three of them went off down the corridor.

Cohen looked keenly at Jarvis as he came back to him. 'Who's the fellow?' he asked.

'Her fiancé,' replied Jarvis brusquely.

Cohen whistled. 'I thought you and she might make a go of it,' he observed.

'Did you?'

Cohen saw the threat in the questioner's eye, and moved to safer topics. 'How d'you fancy Greyhavens on Saturday's match?' he began, but Jarvis dragged him back to business.

'What about the Bruce and Easson deaths?'

Cohen shook his head expressively. 'Nothing to go on.'

Jarvis paused, but Cohen had nothing to add. 'And Imogen?' Jarvis asked.

'She and Maurice were downstairs. She was a major witness.'

'I found I didn't want to read about it.'

'Oh. Well, she was a Crown witness naturally, and stayed in the public benches once she was finished. Didn't you see them?'

'No. I was at the back upstairs. I could barely see the dock.'

'Oh! Do you want to see her? Though I think they've left.'

'No. I don't think we've much to say to each other. Maurice was here too? They got over our visit?' Jarvis said, smiling.

'I should say so! I thought you knew. She married Maurice a couple of months ago. It was in all the papers.'

'Oh! I've been out of the country,' Jarvis explained.

'You must have been to miss it. Some of the tabloids made a splash: "Glamorous Widow" and all that. Though they'd to be careful with the impending trial.'

'But I dare say she's been signed up by one of them for later.'

''Fraid so.' Cohen nodded.

'What are they going to do now?'

Cohen shrugged. 'The Gallery's for sale. But more likely it's closing. She's moved to Paris. Buena Vista's for sale.'

'Maybe I'll go round to the Gallery and see if there are any bargains. As a souvenir. If La Imogen's not there.'

'But you've got one! At least one.'

'Not any more.'

'What've you done with the picture?' asked Cohen.

Jarvis chuckled. 'Ben'd laugh like a drain,' he replied. 'One of the Vice-Principals was round at my place and admired it, so I've presented it to the University. It'll go well with the rest of their collection.'

Cohen cackled and Jarvis joined in.

The constable on duty in the corridor came over and asked them to be a little more quiet as the court had started the next case.

THE END